I0625867

GALAXY
CHRONICLES

ROD J.
SPURGEON

OWN THE ENTIRE STARCRUISER
GALAXY COLLECTION
BY
ROD J. SPURGEON

———

Who Blew Up My Ship?

The Wereghost Menace

A Very Goober Christmas

The Vampire Clones of Clegz

Galaxy Chronicles

Galaxy Diaries

Brakka's Zombie Armada

Galaxy Chronicles

ROD J. SPURGEON

The characters and events portrayed in this book are fictitious. Any similarity to real persons, living or dead, is coincidental and not intended by the author.

Copyright © 2013 Rod J. Spurgeon

All Rights Reserved.

No part of this book may be reproduced or transmitted in any manner without the prior written consent of the publisher, except in the case of brief excerpts in critical reviews or articles.

A Tioran Publishing release.

http://www.starcruisergalaxy.com

CONTENTS

Drone Wars   Pg 1

Hot Lava   Pg 13

Double-Rowed Smile   Pg 27

Drone Wars II   Pg 39

Arms Deal   Pg 54

Stimugen   Pg 68

Discount Dinner   Pg 77

Distant Discovery   Pg 95

Damage Control   Pg 116

Distant Discovery II   Pg 130

Derelict Disaster   Pg 148

Deceptive Cargo   Pg 166

Excerpt from Vampire Clones   Pg 182
of Clegz

About the Author   Pg 188

"Without a crew, a starship is just a useless hunk of metal floating aimlessly in space. How it got that way is no concern of mine. I just salvage it."

— *Unknown Scavenger*

DRONE WARS

Jonn peered into the gloom of a war-ravaged hallway. The once opulent resort hotel was a blackened husk of its former glory, one of the victims of the war between the Tioran Federation and the sentient drone forces of the Free Sapience Liberation Army. While the hotel was one of only a few that remained standing in the rubble-filled city of Kilagra, its charred and pitted walls paired with endless piles of shattered glass to ward away potential visitors.

Power to the hotel was severed more than a week ago when drone forces attacked. Few managed to escape the onslaught of the drone army. Those who survived soon wished they hadn't when they were ultimately captured by drones and augmented with mind-control devices to serve FSLA forces. With the hotel's backup generator now teetering on the verge of collapse, precious little energy remained to power the hotel's control systems, making Jonn's search for survivors all the more difficult.

The black and gold laser rifle in his vice-like grip felt light in his hands. He tensed his trigger finger, ready to fire on any drones that crossed his path. He moved cautiously forward, sidestepping chunks of drywall and glass to make as little noise as possible while searching the 14th floor of the resort for survivors. He paused when the life form detector of his laser rifle picked up three life signs two doors ahead to the right.

With an extreme sense of anxiety roiling in his stomach, Jonn resumed his move forward. He swallowed hard and sucked in a deep breath as he reached for the room's access panel to the left of the door. A faint, flickering yellow light emitted from the panel in response to his touch. He heard the security system attempt to release the locking mechanism of the door, but the available power level was far too low to complete the task. He knew the only way in was to blast his way through the door—a move that was likely to alert any nearby drones to his presence.

He checked the scanner on his rifle once more. The life signs were faint but stable, for now. It was a situation that wouldn't last much longer with the bulk of drone forces on Tioran Prime moving steadily in his direction. There was no choice. He had to act now, or the people stranded on the other side of the door would soon expire.

Setting his weapon on low power and taking careful aim, he blasted a person-sized hole in the door. He charged boldly into the room, throwing caution to the wind as time grew short. Through the dim orange illumination of the emergency lights, he spotted three shadowy figures huddled in a darkened corner of the room. He guardedly raised his weapon toward the figures, preparing for the unexpected.

"Human or drone servant?" Jonn asked in a stern voice. He heard something rustle as one of the figures grew taller. His index finger instinctively began pressing on the trigger button.

"Don't shoot," a male voice called out from the darkness. "We've been trapped here for the last week, since the start of the war. Can you help us?"

Jonn removed his finger from the trigger, but kept the barrel of his rifle pointed toward the man. "Step into the light so I can see you."

The figure leaned down and lifted a smaller figure into his arms. When the three approached, he noticed the man was with a woman and a small child. The family was dirty and looked malnourished, but seemed to be in somewhat reasonable health given their situation.

"Please," the woman said. Her long, curly red hair partially covered the left side of her face. "Our daughter is weak from hunger. Do you have anything she could eat?"

Jonn studied the girl, noticing the gaunt, frail appearance of her face and thin frame. He nodded, opened a pocket in his black vest, and pulled out a nourish bar. He handed the "full meal in a compact bar" to the woman and watched as she broke off a small piece and fed it to the young girl. The 5-year-old responded slowly at first, but quickly perked up as the instant energy component of the bar kicked in.

The woman split the remainder of the bar in half and handed a portion to her husband, consuming the final morsel herself.

"My name is Noah and this is my wife,

Gliza, and our daughter, Krista. Thank you so much for your help. You don't know what this means to us."

Jonn nodded. "It's good to meet you, but we really have to get going. Reconnaissance drones will probably be here soon to investigate the noise from the blast. We don't want to be anywhere near this place when they get here."

"I understand," the man said. He cradled his daughter more tightly in his arms, like a professional sports player holding protectively onto the game ball. "We're ready."

"Good," Jonn replied. "This way."

Jonn stepped carefully into the hallway, searching both sides of the wide, long passage. When he detected no imminent threat, he motioned to the family to follow.

"Which way?" Gliza asked when they were in the hall.

Jonn pointed the barrel of his rifle toward the north end of the hall. "There. Take the emergency exit lift to the ground floor. My shuttle is just outside."

"That's pretty," Krista said. She pointed toward the opposite end of the hallway.

The rest of the group peered into the direction indicated by the girl. A single glowing green point of light hovered above the ground in the gloom.

"What is it?" Noah asked.

A wave of dread washed across Jonn's entire body. He knew the light from the recon drone all too well. More than a dozen other green points rapidly joined the first, forming a small swarm.

"Run!" he shouted at the family.

Gliza grabbed Noah's right hand and pulled him toward the exit. Jonn stood his ground, switching his rifle to maximum rapid pulse fire. He fired a burst toward the swarm of green lights, extinguishing three of them within a matter of seconds. A dozen more drones filled the end of the hall and began moving rapidly in Jonn's direction.

With at least 20 drones bearing down on him, Jonn chased after the family, extending his rifle behind him with his right hand, firing blindly at the drones.

He had only swept the first 14 floors of the 50-story hotel when he discovered the family of three. Now that the drones detected his presence, the mechanical monsters would scour the rest of the building, eliminating anyone they found. He regretted not being able to help anyone else that might still be alive in the hotel, but unless he moved this family out of harm's way, they wouldn't have a chance at survival.

Resolved to save what could be the last three survivors on the planet, he approached the door of the emergency exit and pressed his palm to a panel embedded in the wall.

The emergency exit lift drew its power from an independent emergency source and remained fully operational, for the time being. The door retracted into the wall and a lift platform made up entirely of an opaque, blue energy formed outside.

Jonn stepped onto the platform high above the ground and looked back into the hallway. Light from the waning sun beamed into the hotel through the lift and he could clearly see the drones closing in with nimble speed. The black, egg-shaped beasts each had two tentacle-like arms with a short-range beam blaster at the tip of each one. When they were within range, they unleash a torrent of energy fire at Jonn. Before the beams could strike the Starcruiser Galaxy's programmer, the emergency exit door closed, and the platform dropped with frightening speed to the ground level. Fortunately for Jonn, the platform's inertia compensator still functioned, preventing injury during the rapid fall. When the platform came to an abrupt, but soft landing, it disappeared, leaving him standing on a landing pad next to the hotel.

Before he had a chance to move, the sound of tearing metal from high above grabbed his attention. The drones worked to blast apart the emergency exit door on the 14th floor, determined to hunt down and kill their prey. He looked toward the shuttle and saw the access hatch open with the rescued family secured inside. Noah motioned for him to hurry and then pointed to the right. Jonn looked in the direction indicated and saw a large stalker drone moving in their direction. The heavy fighter flew low above the ground, taking its time to study its prey as it approached.

After a moment's hesitation at the ominous sight, Jonn ran toward the shuttle. He was less than 50 feet away from the small craft when the drone fighter ship launched a single plasma bolt. The green sphere of energy slammed into the yellow and silver eight-person shuttle, completely obliterating the ship. The force of the explosion flung Jonn backward several feet and he landed hard on the desert, water-saving landscaping.

Jonn screamed in pain when he fell on a fist-sized rock that crushed his elbow. He did his best to fight through the agonizing pain and gazed in horror at the burning remains of his ship, and the family he thought he had rescued. The stalker drone moved to within 20 feet above the burning remains of the shuttle and pointed its plasma cannon directly at him.

An explosion from above pulled his attention away from the grisly sight. The recon drones finally punched through the durable, but not indestructible emergency door and quickly descended in his direction. Jonn knew the drone army had transformed many the population into mindless servants to help with the FSLA war efforts. He had no intention of allowing himself to be captured and converted into an obedient slave.

Jonn's rifle had skittered out of reach when he was thrown backward from the shuttle explosion. He lunged for the weapon, grimacing in pain when he grabbed it and rolled on the ground. The programmer brought himself up onto one knee and pointed the rifle directly above him. He blasted apart several recon drones, averting his eyes from the destruction to avoid the shower of debris that rained down on top of him. He froze when he heard the threatening whir of an energy device powering up. He looked toward the shuttle and saw the stalker drone's plasma cannon preparing to fire.

In a final, desperate act of defiance, he redirected his rifle at the stalker drone and pumped as many shots as he could into the mechanical fiend.

"Jonn? Helllllloooo," a familiar, disembodied voice called out.

Jonn looked around the area but couldn't identify the origin of the voice.

The stalker drone suffered moderate damage from his torrent of energy fire, but the unwavering fighter shrugged off the attack and continued its mission to exterminate all life on the planet.

"Are you finished yet, Jonn?" the disembodied voice asked.

Jonn ignored the voice and continued blasting away at the fighter as it fired a high-yield plasma shot in his direction. He closed his eyes at the sight of the energy bolt, waiting for the inevitable. When several seconds passed by without incident, he opened his eyes.

"There you are," Goober said. The communication specialist's nose loitered a few short inches away from Jonn's face. The programmer blinked in surprise.

"You must have been having a lot of fun in there," Goober continued. "The captain's been calling you for the last half hour."

Jonn stared in dumbfounded awe at Goober for a moment before reorienting himself to reality. He was still sitting comfortably in a plush chair in his quarters, safe and sound where he planted himself five hours ago. The Drone Wars simulator was the latest full-immersion game on the market and had absorbed most his free time for the past two weeks. He pulled the small, octagon-shaped sim device from his left temple. "Yeah. I guess I got a little further along in the game than I thought I would."

Goober nodded. "That's good. I never made it past the first level, so I gave up. Anyway, you should see what the captain wants before he gets mad."

"I will," Jonn agreed. He flexed his left arm to make sure it still worked.

"Okay. I'm going to get started on dinner. See you in an hour."

Jonn smiled. "See you then."

After Goober left the room, Jonn stared at the sim device in his hand. He replayed the attack in his head, thinking about how to escape the drone attack at the hotel when a thought occurred to him. "Well, the captain's waited this long. I'm sure he'll be okay waiting a little while longer," he said aloud to himself.

He sat back in his comfortable yellow chair

and placed the sim device on his temple. "I know just how to get you bastards, this time," he said before restarting the Drone Wars sim from a previous save point.

HOT LAVA

The Starcruiser Galaxy's sleek, green hull hovered vertically 100 meters above a massive pool of molten lava on the planet Certos. Neither gaining nor losing altitude, the stalwart cruiser fought desperately to break free of the sudden, cataclysmic shift in planetary tectonic configuration.

"Engines at maximum, Captain!" Jonn shouted in desperation. The Galaxy's programmer did his best to coax every ounce of power he could out of the ship's engines, but the damage they suffered during a recent pirate attack caused them to produce only ten percent of their normal thrust.

"The lava's rising, Captain," Goober said.

He studied his tactical display of the planet in relation to the ship and wasn't encouraged by what he saw. "We have about five minutes until this entire region will be completely consumed by the flow—and us with it."

Steve narrowed his eyes at Jonn. "You just had to pick this planet to finish repairs. Didn't you?" The Galaxy's weapons specialist refused to contribute to the decision to set down on the planet's surface when Jonn suggested it, and felt compelled to remind everyone on the bridge that it wasn't his fault they were in this situation.

"Oh, so now you want to talk about the decision," Hitch's disembodied voice said over the ship's communication system. "If you're so interested in it, then why don't you get your butt down here and help with repairs so we can leave."

"Is that a subtle invitation to spend our last few moments together?" Steve asked with a smirk.

"Only you would think about that at a time like this, you jerk. Never mind. I'll figure it out myself. You'd only end up sticking your microspanner in the wrong place anyway—again."

Steve shifted uncomfortably in his chair. "Look, I already told you, I never met a

Kelarian before. How was I supposed to know that things aren't exactly in their usual places with her people?"

"You should have probably explained your lack of experience to her afterward. Oh wait, that's right. She got a nasty ear infection shortly after meeting you. Well, I'm sure it's cleared up by now, although I doubt she'd want to hear from you again, even if she could."

He opened his mouth to reply but was too embarrassed and angry to say anything intelligible.

Mintax grimaced at the unpleasant exchange of information. "That's enough. We have three minutes to get the heck out of here and I want solutions. Jonn?"

"Well, Captain, I have a suggestion, but you're not going to like it," Jonn said.

Mintax was used to worst-case scenario solutions that either damaged his ship or left him broke at the end of the day. There was no illusion that Jonn's pending solution would be any different. "What is it?"

Jonn swiveled in his green and silver chair to face him. "To get more power to the engines without repairing the damage outside the ship, we have to directly infuse them with raw energy from the Infinity reactor. The unprocessed power flow will give the engines the extra juice they need to overcome structural issues. We just have to make sure to shut them down after a few minutes, or we'll burn out the drive system."

Mintax raised his eyebrows in surprise. He expected a more costly solution and was uncharacteristically pleased by the good news. "Good work. Get it done."

Jonn nodded. "Before I make the changes, there's probably something you'll want to know."

Mintax slumped in his seat. He knew it couldn't be that easy; nothing ever was. "And that is?"

The programmer swallowed, knowing that the next piece of information might be particularly difficult for the crew to digest. "We're going to have to shut down the engines briefly while I reconfigure the power flow."

"Are you freaking nuts?" Steve asked in disbelief. "We'd drop into the lava flow and be incinerated. Are you trying to get us all killed?"

"He has a point, Jonn," Mintax said calmly. "The moment we shut down our engine, the ship will plunge into the lava. We wouldn't stand a chance in that mess down there."

"Sure we would," Goober interjected.

The crew turned to look at him, most of them wondering if he was suffering from the same space sickness Jonn must be.

"The ship's hull is made out of lizanium," he continued. "It's the strongest metal we know about, although it is a little too rare and expensive for most shipbuilders to use in their designs. Anyway, it should hold up for at least a minute or two."

"Should," Mintax repeated. "I really don't like that word. It never works out in my favor."

"It will this time, Captain," Jonn insisted. "It'll only take me 30 seconds to reroute the power flow from my console and we can be up and out of here shortly after that. But it can't be done while the engines are engaged or the sudden disruption will cause their flow regulators to overload and explode. Trust me; it will work."

"What about the shields?" Mintax wanted to know. "Can you get them online?"

"The emitters are still damaged from the pirate attack," Hitch said. "They're not going to help us this time."

Mintax remained silent for a few moments while mulling over the details of the situation. "What do you think, Hitch? Does this plan have a shot at working?"

"It's the only plan we've got, Captain, and we're running out of time. I think we should go for it."

"Thirty seconds until the flow reaches the ship, Captain," Goober announced. "If we're going to do something about it, we'd better do it quick. The lava's about to swallow us up."

"I guess we don't have much of a choice then. Do we?" Mintax asked rhetorically. "We're going in one way or another, and I'd rather it be on our own terms, even if it'll lead to the same conclusion."

"It won't, Captain," Jonn insisted. "I promise."

"Go for it," Mintax ordered.

"Disengaging engines and prepping ignition inducers," Hitch announced.

The engines of the Galaxy continued to struggle mightily against the heavy gravitational pull of the planet for one last moment before shutting down. Without their determined support, the Galaxy fell helplessly toward the intense pool of death awaiting it below.

"Hang on!" Mintax shouted just before the ship plunged into the liquid sea of molten rock.

A spray of searing hot lava splashed high into the air when the aft section of the Galaxy's hull plunged into the reddish-orange sea. The teeth-jarring impact thrust the Galaxy's crew hard against their seats. Jonn entered last-minute configuration data into his console when the collision forced him off balance and out of his seat. His head struck the unpadded side of his chair as he tumbled to the deck and slid along its surface. He rolled unconsciously toward the rear end of the bridge when Mintax's massive, muscular right arm reached out and grabbed Jonn's limp hand. Mintax heard and felt an audible tear in his shoulder when he prevented his programmer from slamming into the rear bulkhead.

"Jonn!" Goober shouted. He flew out of his seat to help his friend.

Mintax endured extreme pain as he held Jonn in place. "Hurry," he said, grimacing in agony.

Steve climbed and pivoted along the floor to help Goober with their fallen comrade. As he did, the ship shifted orientation while sinking at an odd angle into the lava. The combat veteran was used to extreme conditions on the battlefield and managed to adjust his orientation to compensate for the new position. He reached Jonn and helped Goober support him against the twisting alignment of the ship.

Released from the heavy load, Mintax retracted his right arm and immediately clutched his shoulder with his left hand. "How is he?"

"Well, he's alive," Steve said. "That's something, at least."

A piercing alarm sounded on the bridge, warning its occupants of a critical situation.

Steve stared into Goober's eyes. "Go. I've got him."

Goober darted as best he could to his analysis console. "Several sections of the hull have collapsed and lava is pouring into the ship. I've isolated the areas with force fields, but they won't hold for long."

"Captain," Hitch's voice came through the communication system, "if we don't get the engines back online soon, we're never going to. What's Jonn's status?"

Steve looked at Mintax and shook his head. "I don't think he's waking up anytime soon, and there's no time to get him to the med bay. We're on our own."

The captain cursed under his breath, partly for allowing his crew to become endangered in the first place and partly for not being able to devise an alternative solution.

A series of explosions rocked the ship when volatile components were exposed to the extreme temperature of the lava.

"I guess that's it then," Steve said, resigning himself to the inevitable. "Hitch, about earlier, I—."

"I know," she cut in. "Me too."

Goober manipulated and analyzed a series of holographic data screens above his console. "Guys, I've been taking a look at what Jonn was trying to do, and I think I can help."

Mintax and Steve immediately shifted their attention to him.

"Go on," Mintax encouraged, trying not to get his hopes up.

"I can't finish his reprogramming of the reactor system, but I can redirect a source of power right next to the engines."

Steve's face contorted in confusion. "What power?"

"The lava," Goober replied.

Steve deflated at the implausible solution. "I don't think melting the engines is going to help. Thanks for trying."

"Wait," Mintax said to Steve. "Go on, Goober."

"Well," he continued, "if I drop the force field in a section near the engine compartment and use redirection force fields to funnel the flow through the power conduits and into the induction chamber, the system should be able to convert the lava to pure energy before it can melt the system components."

"That's great for the system, but won't the conduits melt and cut off the flow?" Steve asked.

"Maybe not," Hitch interjected, "at least, not right away. They're designed to endure extreme temperatures for high capacity flow from the reactor. They didn't skimp on quality when they put this ship together."

The ship emitted a metal moan of protest as the lava seared the hull.

"Do it," Mintax ordered.

Goober nodded and began entering commands into his console. "I have to redirect the lava flow through junction J4 and into a compartment at the end of the corridor. It'll just take a few seconds."

"Wait, J4?" Mintax asked. "What compartment are you funneling the lava into?"

"Um, the one next to the engine room," Goober replied uncomfortably, knowing Mintax wouldn't like the answer.

"That's my fitness center!" the captain roared. "Is there any *other* route you can use to direct the flow?"

"Maybe, but it would melt a quarter of the ship and we wouldn't have enough time to ignite the engines before the hull gives out. Sorry, Captain, but this is the only way."

"Hitch?" Mintax asked, hoping she could find an alternative solution.

"He's right. It's the quickest route to the engines, Captain. Sorry."

Mintax slapped his forehead in frustration. The worst-case scenario solution just got worse. "Fine. Do it. It's not like we have a choice."

"Yes, Captain," Goober replied.

When he directed the lava flow into the fitness center, Mintax's expensive equipment, purchased only six months prior at a deep discount, disintegrated under the intense heat.

After a few seconds, Goober smiled at his display screen. "It's working, Captain. The lava is being converted into energy."

"Powering up the engines," Hitch announced.

The ship shuddered as its engines roared back to life. The cruiser slowly rose out of the roiling sea, revealing its red-hot hull. Lava poured off the ship and fell back into the pool. Within a matter of seconds, the Galaxy emerged from the lava, denying its adversary a prestigious prize.

When the Galaxy reached orbit, Hitch shut down the engines and purged all remaining lava from the ship into space. Though the lava badly scorched and warped the Galaxy's hull, the ship remained intact, defying the odds of its survival.

"Whew, that was a close one." Steve allowed himself a brief moment to relax on the deck next to Jonn. "Good job, kid. I think you earned yourself a case of StimCap."

"Whoo-hoo!" Goober cheered. "Are you buying?"

"No," Steve answered, "but you sure earned one."

Goober's shoulders sagged. "Great. Thanks."

"I'll buy you a StimCap when we take the ship in for repairs, Goober," Hitch announced over the communication system. "Mr. Generous probably blew all of his money on his date last week."

"And that's supposed to be a bad thing?" Steve asked in mock offense.

Before Hitch could reply, Jonn stirred. "What—. What happened?" He started to sit up, but Steve held him firmly to the ground.

"Easy there," he soothed. "You have a

nasty concussion and you need to rest for a while."

When he reoriented himself beyond his pain, Jonn struggled against Steve's firm hand on his shoulder. "The ship," he remembered. "I have to get the engines working, or we're all dead."

"Relax, kid," Steve said. "Goober took care of it."

Jonn gazed in wonder at Goober. "He did?"

Goober shrugged. "I'm not as good a programmer as you are, but I know the ship isn't ready to give up yet. I just helped it find its path out of danger." He patted his console with appreciative care.

"Wow. Nice job," Jonn praised.

"The job's not done yet," Mintax said. "We have a lot of repair work to get done before we can limp our way to Century Delta Station. Steve, take Jonn to the med bay and take care of his injuries. Hitch, make sure hull integrity is stabilized, and then get the engines back online using normal power. Goober, do what you can to stabilize environmental control in the undamaged sections of the ship, and then help Hitch with repair efforts. I'll contact the station and let them know we're coming. Again."

After Steve and Jonn left the room and Hitch was no longer on the communication system, Mintax turned to face Goober. "You did well today. Good job."

Goober beamed with satisfaction at the unexpected compliment. "Thanks, Captain. Does that mean I can take a break for a while after I finish with environmental control?"

"No, but I'll buy you that case of StimCap when we get to the station."

"All right!" His favorite drink helped enhance his focus and increased his response time during long nights of gaming. He looked forward to enjoying a refreshed supply to fuel his habit, and perhaps, creating a game scenario of his own with a little help from Jonn's programming expertise.

DOUBLE-ROWED SMILE

Steve busily munched on a mouth full of savory eggs as he scooped up another fork full. He was about to plunge the delicious goodness into his mouth when his eyes glanced over at Goober.

Instead of eating his own batch of eggs, the young science and communications specialist aboard the Starcruiser Galaxy pulled down his lower lip with his index finger while staring back at Steve. The unusual gesture unnerved the Galaxy's weapons expert.

Steve grimaced at the sight. "What do you think you're doing?" he asked.

Goober released his lip. "Well, I've noticed that when people smile, they only show their top teeth. I'm seeing if I can smile with both my top and bottom teeth showing. Did it work?"

"It didn't look like it from here," Jonn answered. The gifted programmer sat to the right of Goober and only had a sideways view of the smile. He shifted his position in his chair to face his crewmate, resting his right arm on the polished metal dining table. "Okay. Do it again."

The teenager repeated the gesture, crinkling his nose in the process to give his upper lip extra lift.

A disgusted chill washed over Steve as he watched a repeat performance of the unsettling gesture. "You're a strange kid, Goober."

"And don't ever change," Hitch added. The Galaxy's engineer narrowed her hazel eyes at Steve in admonishment.

Jonn studied Goober's ghoulish smile. "It sort of looks like you're angry about being constipated. You should probably stick with your regular smile."

Goober removed his finger from his lip and nodded. "Yeah. I think you're right. I doubt I could smile like that if my hands were busy with something else anyway."

Steve rolled his eyes. "Yeah. That's a good

reason. Go with that."

Captain Mintax dropped his fork onto his empty plate and stood. "If you kids are done playing with your breakfast, we have a new auto-nav to test out." He looked across the table at Jonn. "Did you finish running the simulation to see if it'll work?"

Jonn pivoted in his seat to face him. "Everything checks out according to design specs, and it performed okay in simulated runs. As far as I can tell, it should work."

"That doesn't exactly sound like a vote of confidence in the thing. What's wrong with it?"

Jonn shrugged. "Well, nothing I can really put my finger on, but it just doesn't feel right. There's a reason most starships don't have autopilots, and I just think we'd be better off finding a real person for the job."

"We've been over this," Mintax said in a stern tone. "Pilots cost money, and that's something we don't have a lot of at the moment. Make it work."

Jonn nodded. "Since I can't talk you out of it, I guess it's ready to go."

"Good, because if it doesn't work, you'll have to continue serving as acting navigator." Mintax turned and walked toward the exit of the Stargazers Lounge. "I expect all of you at your posts in ten minutes. We're going to see if this thing was worth the money we paid for it."

After the captain had left the room, Goober flashed a curious look at Hitch. "Didn't we get the auto-nav for free from a derelict ship?"

"You mean that broken wreck we found floating around an asteroid field in a million pieces?" Steve asked.

"Yes. We did," Hitch answered, ignoring the weapons expert's snarky question.

Goober exhaled audibly. "I hope it works better for us than it did for them."

Steve stood and dropped his soiled napkin on the table. "That's something to look forward to. We'd better get going. Our fate awaits us in however many pieces it so chooses."

* * *

Mintax adjusted his massive, muscular girth to a more comfortable position in his command chair. The bridge of the Galaxy was spacious, laced with deep green plating and silver accents, but years of heavy battle damage and cosmetic neglect had left it in desperate need of a facelift. "Engage when ready," he ordered.

Jonn tapped on the controls of the navigation station directly in front of the captain. "All right, I've laid in the new course to Oikko V. It's near an outpost with a medical facility, just in case this doesn't go well."

Mintax growled.

"Just kidding," Jonn assured. "I hope," he added in a soft whisper. He pressed a glowing green circle on the holographic controls and sat back in his seat, bracing himself against any unforeseen perils.

A stream of data and star charts moved rapidly across the navigational control screen, faster than any unaugmented person could control. The processing and analysis performed by the auto-nav were visually stunning, impressing the entire crew.

After a few moments of careful analysis, a spatial rift formed in front of the Galaxy, pulling the stalwart green vessel inside.

Jonn analyzed the results of the shift to warp and smiled. "It looks like we're perfectly on course to Oikko V, Captain. This might actually work out, after all."

Goober studied the main viewscreen and tilted his head to the right. "Is it me or are we a little crooked?"

"We might take what we need from time to time, but I wouldn't exactly call us crooked," Steve replied.

Goober shook his head. "Yeah. I guess so, but that's not what I'm talking about. Look." He pointed at the viewscreen.

The crew scrutinized the viewer, searching for what the young communications specialist was referring to.

It took Jonn a few moments of careful inspection to notice the slight imperfection in the angle of the warp. His eyes opened wide in shock, and he began tapping furiously on the navigation console.

"What is it now?" Mintax asked in a flat voice. He knew better than to hope for the best, given their less than positive history with luck. Despite his experience, he was still optimistic that at least something would work out in his favor, just this once.

He was wrong.

The ship turned slowly, but noticeably to the right, shifting toward a more perpendicular angle to the warp tunnel as they traveled through it. When the angle became more pronounced, the Galaxy began vibrating, as though encountering minor turbulence.

Jonn continued working feverishly at the

navigational controls. "Captain, the auto-nav isn't compensating for warp drift. If I can't correct our angle, the ship is going to be ripped apart."

Mintax leaned forward in stone cold seriousness, his hands gripping the arms of his chair. "Then shut the damn thing off."

"That's just it," Jonn continued. "The auto-nav won't release the controls until we're safely through the warp tunnel at our destination."

"How long until we get there?" Hitch asked.

Jonn studied his control screen. "Another four minutes."

"Can we make it that far?" Steve asked.

Mintax knew the answer before the programmer could reply.

"No. I'm trying to hack the lock-out," Jonn said, tapping furiously at his console. "It's the only way to get access to the navigation controls, but I need more time."

Hitch ran over to him and studied the control screen. "What can I do to help?"

Jonn shook his head. "Nothing. If I can't get access to the system to stop the warp in time, we're not going to make it."

Steve crossed his arms in frustration. "I guess now we know why the auto-nav's previous owners lost their ship. Didn't I say this was a bad idea?"

Mintax didn't remove his eyes from Jonn's work. "That's not helping, Steve."

The ship shuddered more violently, causing the crew to brace their positions to remain stable.

Steve sighed. "I always knew this ride wouldn't last forever. I guess I just expected us to go out in a blaze of glory against impossible odds, not some stupid warp accident."

"We're not dead yet," Mintax said.

"I'm almost there, Captain," Jonn said, continuing his attempt to hack his way into the navigation system.

Hitch watched the programmer's progress and knew he wouldn't finish his work in time. She turned slowly toward Mintax.

The captain pinched his eyebrows together in a concerned, questioning stare.

She shook her head slightly in response to the silent query.

Minax sat back in his chair and softened his expression at his engineer. His eyes studied her silky, jet black hair and soft facial features before locking with her hazel eyes. He never allowed their unspoken interest in each other to develop and potentially interfere with their jobs or their friendship. He began to question that decision as they faced imminent destruction.

Goober studied a schematic of the navigation system on his scientific analysis station when an idea popped into his head. "Captain, if we can't shut down the auto-nav, couldn't we just disconnect it? It is just a module, isn't it?"

Mintax stared at his programmer expectantly.

Jonn shook his head. "If we try to remove it, its security protocols will detect the intrusion and scramble the access encryption of the nav system. We'll be exactly where we are now with no way to access the controls. I have to gain access to the system first to disable its embedded security."

"What would happen if you yanked it out fast?" Goober asked. "Couldn't you just pull it out before it has a chance to lock out the controls?"

Jonn shook his head. "I doubt it. The module can respond faster to tampering attempts than it would take us to pull it out. It might be our best bet at this point though. I don't think I can crack the system in time."

"Do it," Mintax ordered.

Jonn exhaled audibly, hoping his agility

wouldn't let him and the rest of the crew down. "I'll try, Captain."

Steve stood, bracing his stance against the turbulence by gripping the green padding of his chair. "Get out of the way." He pulled his silver pulse pistol from its holster, activated its power core, and aimed it at the navigation console.

The crew looked over at Steve and saw what he intended. Mintax, Jonn and Hitch immediately scattered just before a blue bolt of energy from the man's pistol blasted apart the navigation console. Debris flew across the bridge, covering the command center of the Galaxy in a shower of small metal and electronic fragments. The ship's safety protocols immediately kicked in, instantly dropping it out of warp. After a few seconds, the Galaxy came to a dead stop, ending the tumultuous ride.

Hitch stood and brushed console fragments off her clothes. "How about a little warning next time?"

Steve deactivated the power core of his pistol and placed it back in its holster. "You're welcome."

Mintax wiped a thin layer of console debris from his bald head and black t-shirt. "Status report."

Goober activated the ship's status screen on his console. "We're stopped, Captain."

"No kidding." Steve's voice dripped with sarcasm.

"What about the ship, Goober?" Mintax calmly inquired.

"Oh. Right. Other than the navigation console, the ship seems to be okay."

"No thanks to the auto-nav," Steve added. "Maybe we can spring for an actual pilot now." He raised a scolding eyebrow at Mintax as though to say, "I told you so."

"You just volunteered for the job until we find a replacement," Mintax responded.

"Aw, heck," Steve said, grumbled at the thought of enduring the tedious job.

Hitch smiled at the weapons expert as he sunk miserably into his chair.

Jonn moved to the weapons control console. "I'll reroute navigational controls to your station until we can rebuild the nav console."

Steve crossed his arms and watched as Jonn tapped on the controls at his station. "Great. Thanks."

Hitch moved closer to Mintax. "For a minute there, I didn't think we were going to make it." She stared into his green eyes, hoping to see the spark of interest she thought she saw just a few short moments ago.

Mintax wanted to hug her to celebrate their survival, but he knew he might not be able to limit his affection if he lowered his guard against his own emotions. He chose the only response he could think of to deflect the delicate moment. "Death doesn't have a chance against us as long as we have Goober's double-rowed smile warding it away."

Goober turned away from his console, pulled his bottom lip down with his index finger, and flashed his ghoulish smile at the crew.

Hitch smiled at him and then looked back at Mintax. She nodded, knowing that he was hiding from his own emotions by shifting the subject of their conversation to Goober. If they were meant to be together, it wouldn't be this day.

DRONE WARS II

Captain Mintax raised his rifle, sighted his target, and pressed the trigger button. A blue plasma burst launched from the assault weapon and bolted down the long, green hallway.

A black, egg-shaped drone hovered in the air at the opposite end of the corridor tracking the movements of the Starcruiser Galaxy's crew when it detected the impending threat. It darted out of the path of the approaching blast, deftly removing itself from the calculated trajectory. The plasma burst noted the altered location of its target and adjusted its course to compensate. The drone did its best to move itself out of harm's way once more, but it was too late. The plasma burst slammed into the drone, obliterating the tiny craft.

"See? I told you these new rifles were awesome," Steve commented, stroking the black and chrome barrel of the gun as if it was his favorite pet.

Mintax shot a skeptical glance at his weapons expert before he returned his attention to the shattered remains of the drone. "You never did tell me how much they cost."

Steve knew the captain wouldn't approve of the purchase price, so he quickly changed the subject. "We should probably concentrate on getting rid of these drones before they take over the ship." He looked over his shoulder at Jonn. "How many of these things did you say there were?"

Mintax growled and assumed that his weapons specialist grossly overpaid for the four new rifles. If there was one thing the thrifty captain hated more than anything, it was paying more than his perceived value for something, regardless of actual worth.

Jonn cut into the man's thoughts. "I only created one prototype, but it reprogrammed the assembler to create more."

"So you don't know how many there are?"

Mintax asked in annoyance.

Jonn shook his head. "Sorry, Captain."

"That's okay," Goober interjected. "They're not armed like the ones in the game. It shouldn't be too hard to get rid of them."

Jonn rubbed the back of his neck and looked at the Galaxy's communications specialist with a pained expression. "Well, they're probably not going to stay that way."

"What's that supposed to mean?" Mintax asked, uncertain whether he wanted to know the answer.

Jonn inhaled deeply before explaining. "I patterned the drone after the game Drone Wars. You know, the one I've been spending a lot of my free time playing?"

Mintax glared.

"Um, anyway," Jonn continued, "I thought we could use a drone on this ship to help with maintenance and, you know, to keep me company."

"You made yourself a pet?" Steve said.

Jonn nodded. "Sort of, yeah. I extracted the base code from the game's program and used that as a starting point to create a simple artificial intelligence for the drone. I wanted it to look and feel like the drones in the game but without the killer instinct."

Three drones appeared at the end of the

corridor and scanned the remains of their companion. The single, glowing eye at the tip of their bodies turned a darker shade of green as they focused their attention on the Galaxy's crew. Each of the drone's dual tentacles pointed at their new enemy and fired a barrage of yellow laser bursts.

The crew ducked behind the safety of the T-junction walls to avoid the incoming fire.

"I thought you said you programmed them without a killer instinct?" Steve contended.

Jonn swallowed nervously. "I did, and I didn't. Their base program came with three settings: unarmed and unshielded, armed and unshielded, and armed and shielded. They were meant to give a player progressively more difficult levels to choose from in the game. I kept them in the drone's program, just in case we needed it to help us repel intruders, but I set the prototype at level 1. I don't know what happened."

"Your pet grew teeth," Mintax said. "What other surprises should I expect?"

"If they follow the progression of the game, then they probably just upgraded to level two. That means we can still take them out."

"What happens if they get to level three?" Goober asked.

"That would be bad," Jonn said. "Our weapons probably wouldn't penetrate their shields, at least not right away."

Steve steadied his rifle. "Then let's take these bastards out before that happens." He looked at the captain and nodded.

Mintax and Steve moved into the hall, sighted their targets, and fired a series of bursts from their plasma rifles. The drones spotted their prey and returned fire. One of the laser blasts struck Mintax's left arm before he and Steve could return to the safety of the junction. A fraction of a second later, they heard several explosions as the plasma bursts annihilated their targets.

Goober peeked around the corner and inspected the damage. "You got 'em, Captain." He looked at Mintax and saw a small hole with singed edges in his brown shirt. "Captain, you're shot."

"I'm fine," Mintax said through gritted teeth. He narrowed his eyes at Jonn. "Where's your assembler?"

"Engineering."

"That's three decks down," Steve said in disbelief. "Holy crap, they're trying to take over the damn ship if they made it all the way up here."

Mintax moved into the corridor to trace the

direction of the drones. "Then we're going down there to take them out before that happens."

"We should probably fix your arm first," Goober commented, bringing attention back to the captain's arm.

Mintax shook his head. "Later. I want that assembler destroyed and those drone bastards off my ship first."

"Once we get to engineering, I can shut down the assembler and purge the drone's design specs." Jonn assured. "If we're lucky, we can—."

"No!" Mintax interrupted. "The code is still in that damn thing, and I want it destroyed. Is that clear?"

Jonn's shoulders slumped. He spent six weeks creating the nano-assembler to help him design and construct his prototype creations. He wasn't at all happy to learn of its imminent destruction. "But Captain, if I purge the program from the device, we can still use it to create other new technologies."

"If that technology is anything like these drones of yours, no thanks," Steve said.

Mintax shook his head. "I'm not taking any chances. When we get to engineering, we're taking it out."

"Yes, Captain," Jonn responded in

disappointment.

The crew slowly walked to the intra-ship transport chamber at the end of the corridor and moved inside.

"Hmm, that's odd." Goober scratched the side of his head in confusion.

"What is?" Steve asked.

Mintax moved to enter the sequence for transport to engineering.

"Well, if they're as smart as they are in the game, you'd think the drones would try to stop us from getting to engineering. That is their base of operations, so to speak. Isn't it?"

Mintax paused before tapping the final button on the chamber control pad. "He's right. Those bastards probably have a trap waiting for us when we get there."

"Good," Steve replied. "With all of those things clustered in one area, it'll be hard for even Goober to miss."

Goober folded his arms indignantly and grunted. "Humph."

"Yeah, and it'll be hard for them to miss us too," Mintax added.

Steve sighed. "Fine. Then if we can't blast our way through them, I've got another idea that might just do the trick."

* * *

When the crew returned to the bridge, Steve moved back into the intra-ship transport chamber with a pyramid-shaped device he retrieved from his quarters. He kneeled in the chamber and set the device on the floor. With the fingers on his left hand secretly crossed behind his back, he pressed a sequence of buttons on the pyramid's small control screen with his right. The tip of the device opened and expanded outward, orbiting the base of the unit in a counter-clockwise motion.

"Yes!" Steve cheered. He stood, slapped his hands together, and turned to face the rest of the crew on the bridge. "All right, I think it's set."

Mintax raised his left eyebrow in question. "You *think* it's set?"

Steve exited the chamber. "Well, yeah. I bought three trashed versions of those things and barely managed to use them all to build one. We're lucky I finished the project last week."

"What's it supposed to do?" Goober asked.

"If I'm right," Jonn said, "that's a tech II Allari device. I haven't seen one in five years, but essentially, it's designed to reduce a decommissioned ship to its base components for recycling. That was before we started using targeted deconstruction beams, of course."

Goober looked at Steve in concern. "So, we're going to beat the drones by destroying the ship?"

Everyone stared at Steve, waiting for an explanation.

He looked upon the apprehensive expressions of each of his crewmates. "Come on, guys. Do you really think I'd blow us up just to win a fight?"

A thick silence filled the air.

He rested his hands on his hips and frowned. "Well, I wouldn't."

Mintax wasn't entirely convinced. "Uh-huh."

"Look, Jonn built a discriminating isolator for me a few weeks ago, so I can set a specific target parameter. I just set it to target drones, and that's all it will disassemble. Honest. It's a sure thing."

Jonn nodded. "He's right. It should work. Oh, and Captain, I used the assembler to create the discriminator, though I didn't really know what it was for at the time. So, before you destroy the technology that will help us defeat the drones, keep that in mind. Okay?"

Mintax glanced at Jonn to determine the

truthfulness of his statement and returned his attention to Steve. "Do it."

"Now we're talking," Steve said in excitement. He entered the transport chamber, tapped in a delayed detonation on the control screen of the Allari device, and then entered a five-second delay on the transport control panel. After he had exited the chamber, the door closed.

"How are we going to know if it worked?" Goober asked.

A small explosion briefly rocked the ship.

Mintax growled in irritation at his weapons specialist.

Steve smiled to ease the intensely fierce gaze the captain beamed in his direction. "I think it worked."

Jonn moved to the transport door and studied a readout on its external control panel. "Captain, there's a chamber malfunction on the engineering level. We're going to have to use the maintenance access shaft to enter."

"I'm sure it's just a minor glitch," Steve said quickly to ward off harsh criticism.

Goober looked at Jonn to verify Steve's assumption.

The Galaxy's programmer slowly shook his head.

"Well, let's get down there," Mintax

directed in anger. "So help me, if you took out engineering…"

"I'm sure it's fine, Captain," Goober assured. "We probably wouldn't have power if Steve blew up engineering."

"Yeah. He's right," Steve concurred. "See? I told you it would work."

Mintax stepped into the transport chamber and removed an access panel on its rear wall. "I'll believe that when I see it."

* * *

When the crew assembled in the main corridor of the engineering deck, they surveyed the massive collection of drone parts strewn about haphazardly on the floor. They also noticed the singed walls of the corridor.

"Steve," Mintax roared.

Steve raised his hands in a "what" gesture. "So the walls can use a little scrubbing. The plan worked. Didn't it?"

"Captain," Goober interrupted. "The door to engineering is still sealed. Do you think the Allari device affected the drones in there too?"

Mintax looked to Jonn for an answer.

"I doubt it," he replied. "It's a heavy blast door. If it's still intact, then any drones that were in engineering before the blast are unaffected."

Mintax raised his rifle to eye level, ready for combat. "Then let's finish this."

Steve positioned his left hand on the door control panel and used his right to keep his rifle pointed toward the door. He focused his attention on Mintax, waiting for the go signal.

Mintax directed his gaze to the door in front of him and nodded.

When Steve opened the door to engineering, both he and Mintax rushed inside and launched homing plasma bursts from their rifles.

Only five drones remained in engineering to defend the assembler, and the homing plasma bursts completely obliterated four of them. The fifth drone quietly slipped away without detection into the emission transfer duct laced with heavy radiation shielding.

"Is that all of them?" Mintax asked.

Jonn moved to an engineering console and scanned the deck. "I'm not picking up any others on the ship. I think we got them all."

"Not quite," Steve said. "Look." He pointed to a small platform with a rear mounted inverted U arch on the ground next to Jonn's workstation. A mass of gold dust swirled over the assembler, forming into the shape of a drone.

Mintax pointed his rifle at the device. "I'll take care of that."

"Captain, wait," Jonn cried, but it was too late.

The assembler exploded into a shower of parts from the energy pulse of Mintax's rifle.

Jonn sighed in resignation.

Mintax lowered his weapon and pointed two fingers of his left hand at Steve and Jonn. "I expect you two to clean this mess up before Hitch gets back from her supply run. She's going to want her engine room the way it was before she left, and you two better make it happen. Understood?"

"Yes, Captain," Jonn replied.

"I'm sure Jonn can take care of it," Steve said. "I've got to get going. I have a hot date on Polari Station in a couple of hours, and I'd hate to be late." He started moving toward the door.

Mintax narrowed his eyes. "Tell her you're going to be late. You're not going anywhere until this mess is cleaned up."

Steve stopped in his tracks and swiveled back around. "But Captain—."

"Now, Steve."

"Bah," Steve griped. "I hope you know you're ruining my love life, Captain. What if she's the one?"

"I'm sure she is…this week," Mintax answered in reference to Steve's preference for at least one new date every week.

"I think you're just jealous," Steve said, though he knew the captain was right.

Mintax grunted. "That'll be the day."

"I'll help, guys," Goober volunteered. "Maybe you can still see her if we get it done in time."

"Thanks, Goober," Steve said. "I appreciate the help. Too bad more people aren't like you." He glanced at Mintax for a moment before stomping to an engineering console.

The captain shook his head. "Three hours, gentlemen. That's how long you have until Hitch gets back. Good luck." He left the room to return to the bridge.

"Easy for him to say," Steve grumbled. "He's not the one doing the work."

"He's the captain," Goober replied. "If he doesn't watch the bridge, who will?"

"He's got a point," Jonn agreed.

"Yeah, well," Steve said, unwilling to give in to their point of view. "We'd better get going. I have a date to get to."

While the crew worked to restore engineering, the prototype drone entered a small emission exhaust port and escaped from the Galaxy, fleeing the hazards of its birthplace in search of new breeding ground.

ARMS DEAL

Steve pointed a bulky, black rifle at a distant storage container. The empty, semi-metallic box was among several that had been stacked in a corner and forgotten long ago in the cargo bay of the Starcruiser Galaxy. The captain wasn't likely to miss one or two if Steve used them as target practice, at least not right away.

The new pulse weapon felt heavy in his hands, a perfect compensator for what was probably going to be significant recoil. The Galaxy's weapons specialist swiveled his head to the right and smirked at a bearded man standing a few feet away. He returned his gaze to the container and tensed his trigger finger, savoring the rush of excitement that coursed through his body. When his eager finger didn't find what it was looking for, he tilted the rifle at an angle to examine its configuration.

"What the heck?" Steve asked in confusion. "Where's the damn trigger button?"

The arms merchant smugly adjusted his brown vest with angular yellow threading. "I wondered how long it would take you to figure that out." He reached into one of the many pockets of his vest and pulled out a small, crescent-shaped object. The device, roughly half the size of the man's thumb, looked like any other neural computer interface. He placed it behind the back of his right ear and smiled at his customer.

The unexpected action caused Steve's predatory instincts to kick into high alert. He was extremely suspicious of smiling merchants. From previous and usually unpleasant experiences, it was often a telltale sign that either he was about to get a raw deal or the other party had no intention of keeping up his end of the bargain. Judging by the sinister glint in the merchant's eyes, he assumed the latter.

With casual ease, Steve slowly shifted his hands to the business end of the rifle, intending to use it as a blunt weapon should his instincts prove correct.

The merchant noticed the defensive posture and laughed. "What's the matter? Don't trust me?"

Steve tightened his grip around the barrel. "Let's just say I'd rather be safe than sorry. Now, how about explaining to me just exactly what that thing controls."

"I was hoping you'd ask."

Long, black tentacles suddenly sprang out of the rifle. They swiftly wrapped around Steve's entire body, squeezing it in an uncomfortably tight embrace.

"It's the latest design in self-defense weaponry," the merchant said. "What do you think?"

Steve tried to free his hands from the crushing grip of the tentacles, but he was too tightly bound to do more than wiggle his fingers. "Get this off of me!"

"You wouldn't want to buy something before you know its full capabilities. Would you?"

One of the tentacles pointed its sharp, needle-like end directly at Steve's right eye. It moved to within two inches of its target before coming to a stop.

"This is so much more than a basic pulse

rifle, as I'm sure you've figured out by now." The merchant pulled a blue disk from another pocket in his jacket. "It's completely controlled from the neural interface with a range of almost 5,000 meters. I really haven't had a chance to test it beyond that range, but maybe I'll get around to it someday."

Steve's eyes quickly scanned the cargo bay, search for anything that could help him out of his predicament, but nothing immediately stood out. "Some demonstration. How the heck am I supposed to buy the damn thing like this?"

The merchant rubbed his chin and nodded slowly. "Well, you see, the price has gone up a little since we last spoke. I didn't think you were the kind of guy who'd appreciate the full value of a special weapon like that, so I had to take precautions. You know how it is."

"How much more?" Steve grunted.

"I'm going to need 500,000 credits to part with that beauty. It's the only one like it in the galaxy, so I'm sure you can understand its extraordinary value. You wouldn't have asked me here otherwise. Right?"

"We agreed on 100,000, and that's all you're going to get," Steve said through clenched teeth.

The merchant shook his head. "Hmm, no,

that's not going to do."

The tentacles searched Steve's pockets at the cognitive request of its master, but came up empty.

"You don't even have the 100,000 we agreed to." The merchant sounded surprised.

"Ha!" Steve shouted. "So, you admit we agreed on 100,000."

The merchant narrowed his eyes. "Where's the money?"

"You'll never find it, so take your toy and get off this ship. We're done here."

The merchant sighed. "I really wish you hadn't said that." He pressed a blue crystal in the center of the ominous-looking disk in his left hand. An eerie blue glow emitted from the crystal and pulsed outward along thin tracts to the perimeter of the disk. "My time is very valuable and I have no intention of coming all this way for nothing." He extended his left arm and opened his hand. The disk immediately flew across the hangar and attached itself to the wall.

"What the heck was that?" Steve demanded.

"That's controlled by the same interface that allows me to manipulate the rifle. I'll throw it in for free just to show you there are no hard feelings. Now, about my money."

"Money is going to be the least of your problems when the captain shows up. You didn't think I was on this ship by myself. Did you?"

The merchant shrugged. "It doesn't really matter. If I don't get what I came for, you'll lose this ship, and I'll just salvage the wreckage for whatever value I can get out of it. It's a win-win proposition for me. Now, as for you, I think you have an important decision to make. It sounds like an easy one to me, but hey, maybe you don't value your life as much as I do mine."

Steve squinted at the blue pulsing device across the room. "I take it that's some kind of bomb?"

The merchant clapped. "See? You're not so dumb after all."

Steve growled. "Why don't you unbind me? I'll show you how smart I can be."

"Aw, now there you go again. Just when I think we're making progress."

A tentacle slapped Steve across the left side of his face. Hate filled his eyes as a trickle of blood streamed from a cut across his cheek.

"Look, I really can't stay here all day, so if you could hurry this along, I'd really appreciate it," the merchant said.

Steve knew the merchant had every

intention of following through on his threat. This particular individual had come highly recommended by an acquaintance of a black market arms dealer he occasionally dealt with. If he survived this encounter, he would have to pay this acquaintance a special visit to express his heartfelt ingratitude.

"Fine, but you'll have to let me access my comm to have one of my colleagues bring it down."

The merchant waved his hand dismissively. "Whatever. I know you won't try anything so long as the fate of your ship rests on a single thought." He pointed to the device behind his ear.

"Then, do you mind loosening my wrists a little so I can reach my wristcom?"

"Of course."

The tentacles around Steve's wrists slackened just enough for him to access the black wristcom band around his left wrist. He activated its holographic control screen and tapped in a sequence of commands. After a few moments, Goober's smiling face appeared on screen.

"Hi, Steve. Did you finish your deal?"

"Actually, that's why I'm calling. It's a little more expensive than I thought it was, so I need you to pull 500,000 credits from the captain's private stash and bring it down."

Goober knew Captain Mintax had nowhere near that amount hidden anywhere, and was absolutely certain Steve knew that as well. "500,000? Are you sure?"

Steve smiled. "I'm positive. Grab it, and get down here as soon as you can."

Goober nodded. "Okay. If you say so."

Before he terminated the link, Steve managed to tap two words on the holographic control screen without being detected. When he ended the call, the crushing grip of the tentacles once again wrapped themselves tightly around his wrists.

"See? Now, that wasn't so hard. Was it?"

"You'll get what's coming to you. I'll make sure of that."

The merchant didn't appreciate the implication, but he kept his cool. "You're right. I will. Until I warp away safely in my own ship, I can still destroy yours."

"What guarantee do I have that you won't destroy it once you have your money?"

"I may be a little more unconventional in my methods than some of my associates, but killing customers is usually bad for business. Well, unless it's absolutely necessary, of course." He flashed an evil grin.

"Yeah. I bet."

* * *

After a few minutes of tension-filled silence, Goober entered the bay. He spotted Steve entwined by black tentacles and a man with a spiked black and red Mohawk. Both gazed expectantly in his direction.

"Is that my money?" The merchant pointed at him.

He looked down at the small, metallic box in his hands and then looked up at Steve, who nodded at him.

"I guess it is." He moved in the merchant's direction.

"That's far enough," the merchant said.

Goober paused mid-step. "Don't you want to see what's inside?"

The merchant smiled at the teen and pulled a silver, scarab-shaped device from a vest pocket. He held the ornately designed object in his hand and watched as it sprouted long, thin legs. When it finished unfolding itself, the scarab sprang into the air and flew toward Goober. Pausing only when it reached its target, the drone snatched the box out of the man's hands and returned it to the waiting merchant. When it finished its mission, the drone landed comfortably on its master's right shoulder and waited for further instructions.

With eager anticipation, the merchant gripped the lid of the box and paused, directing a cold stare at Steve. "If it's not all here, you might as well say goodbye to your friend, right now. It's the last time you'll see him in one piece."

Feeling confident in his position of power, the merchant flipped the lid open. The micro-electronic destabilizer hidden inside immediately activated, releasing a pulse wave that shut down all independently powered devices in the bay.

The scarab instantly deactivated and fell off the merchant's shoulder, crashing onto the deck. The black market profiteer shifted his gaze from the box to the scarab. "What did you do?" He shot a threatening look at Goober and pulled out an energy pistol hidden in the waistband behind his back.

"That's probably not going to work either," Goober said casually. He noticed Steve struggling against the tentacles and ran over to help.

The tentacles had slackened somewhat and appeared disoriented from the pulse wave, but they managed to maintain access to a source of energy independent from the rifle's power core. Steve struggled to remove one of the writhing appendages from around his waist. "Shouldn't this damn thing be dead like all the other electronics around here?"

Goober looked closely at one of the tentacles. "It looks organic. I think it's alive." He helped Steve slip out from the loosened grasp of the gyrating tentacles and then backed away from the undulating mess.

Removed from distraction, the creature separated itself from the rifle, revealing a small, black body that quickly expanded.

"We should probably get out of here now," Goober suggested, backing toward the exit.

Steve watched in bewilderment as the creature stood vertically on its tentacles and opened a mouth three feet wide. It secreted a blue-flecked black ooze from its mouth, salivating at the tempting morsels that surrounded it.

"Uh, yeah," Steve said. "We're outta here." Steve and Goober bolted toward the exit.

Freed from the confines of its cage under the control of the merchant's neural device, the creature reasserted itself and swiftly adapted to its surroundings. Its instinct to absorb the life force of living beings quickly locked onto the closest source of food it could find.

"Nooo!" Steve heard as he left the hangar.

He turned back in time to see the creature wrap its arms around the merchant and pull the struggling man against its mouth. A thin tube extended from the creature's massive orifice and plunged into the profiteer's chest. The merchant's body shriveled rapidly as the creature sucked him dry.

Steve smiled malevolently at the spectacle. "That's what you get for trying to screw with me, you bastard."

While the creature drained its food, it began to develop an anti-glow, absorbing all light around it as it simultaneously grew in size. When it finished its meal, the black beast discarded the used body and turned its hungry mouth toward the other two men.

"Uh-oh," Goober said when he noted the creature zeroing in on its next victims. He pressed the control panel next to the door and sealed off the bay. "We should probably let the captain know what happened so we can figure out what to do with that." He pointed his thumb at the door.

"I know exactly what to do with it," Steve said. He entered a series of commands into the door's control panel and watched its visual display as the outer bay door opened. The atmosphere inside the bay jettisoned into space, taking the creature, the merchant's shriveled body, and a small collection of empty storage containers with it.

"There. I think that takes care of it," Steve said. He entered the command to reseal and pressurize the hangar.

"Don't you think that was a little mean?" Goober asked. "It was just trying to survive."

Steve gaped at him. "It was going to eat us. What would you have us do with it?"

He shrugged. "I don't know. Maybe drop it off at the nearest uninhabited planet?"

Steve shook his head and smiled. "Your compassion's going to get you into some serious trouble one of these days, Goober. Lucky for you, I'm here to pull your butt out of the fire when you get in a jam."

"Didn't I just save you in there?"

"Yeah, well, we should probably get back to the bridge," Steve said, avoiding the truth of his fallibility. "The captain's going to want to know why we just spaced his ancient storage containers, though I think the new, long-range we just got him will make up for the loss. I don't think its previous owner will need it."

As Steve turned toward the intra-ship transport chamber, he paused. "You did good back there. Thanks. I owe you one."

Goober beamed a bright smile at the back

of Steve's head as the weapons specialist sauntered confidently down the hallway.

STIMUGEN

"Are you sure you're okay?" Goober asked with concern. "You don't look so good."

Hitch's normally calm and calculating demeanor had become more erratic over the past few days. Her long, black hair appeared disheveled and covered most of her face. The usual healthy tan of her skin now looked ghostly white. The Starcruiser Galaxy's engineer was not at all herself these days, and it showed.

Hitch sighed in frustration and turned away from her work repairing a micro-servo control module. She stared directly into Goober's eyes. "For the last time, I'm fine. Now, would you get out of here so I can finish this?" She turned back to her work and ignored the young science and communications specialist.

Goober stared at her in silence for several seconds before responding. "Okay. I brought you some lunch, just in case you were hungry. I haven't seen you in the lounge for the past couple of days, and I thought you could use a bite." He waited for a response, but Hitch didn't offer one.

"I'll just leave this on the table over here," Goober continued. He set down a plate stacked with a triple-decker sandwich and left engineering.

Hitch didn't hear him, choosing instead to lose herself in her work, oblivious to her surroundings. After a few minutes, she furrowed her brow at the small, metallic sphere in her hand. The obstinate device triggered a violent rage deep within Hitch. She did her best to control it, poking inside an access port on the module's side, but her shaking hands prevented her from performing the delicate manipulation required. Suddenly, she tightened her grip on the delicate object, turned around, and threw it across the room.

The device crashed into a green wall just a few short feet away from the exit where Captain Mintax stood. He shielded his eyes when the object exploded in a shower of electronic fragments.

Hitch's anger immediately subsided at the sight of his imposing figure blocking the exit door. "I—I didn't hear you come in."

"Obviously." He walked with casual ease toward her. "Goober told me he thought something might be wrong. Is something bothering you?"

Hitch's eyes flashed with anger at Goober's indiscretion. She balled up her fists as her anger returned. "That little twerp should mind his own damn business."

Mintax's mouth uncharacteristically gaped open at Hitch's surprisingly harsh words. He stared into her eyes, examining them for any revealing signs that might explain her behavior. "When was the last time you had some rest?"

She waved her hand dismissively. "I'm fine."

"Really? Someone who's fine doesn't curse her friends and throw objects around the room."

"I told him I was fine, and he wouldn't leave it alone." Hitch stood rigidly, leaning slightly forward in an aggressive posture as though preparing for battle. "Goober just had to run to you and blab about his false assumptions. Didn't he? He deserves whatever he gets."

Mintax shook his head in disappointment. "Are you listening to yourself right now? This isn't like you." He flashed on the memory of Hitch telling him about a particularly difficult time in her life before she began a fresh start on the Galaxy. The symptoms of her experiences then were similar to the ones she seemed to be suffering from now. "Are you taking Stimugen again?"

Her eyes opened wide at his presumption and she folded her arms tightly against her body. "That's none of your business."

Mintax took her overly defensive response as confirmation of his suspicions. "That stuff was banned by the government for a reason, Hitch. Injectable sleep might keep your body refreshed, but it tears apart your mind. Do you remember telling me about what it did to you when you couldn't find a job years ago? Staying awake for weeks at a time, moving from one cesspool outpost to another." He shook his head. "It put you into a med facility for an entire month and almost damaged your mind beyond restoration. I don't want to see you head down that dark path again."

She turned her back to him as she recalled her difficult past. "I can handle it. I'm only taking partial doses this time."

"Your actions right now are telling me otherwise."

Hitch spun around on her heel and glared into his eyes. "Who else is going to prevent this ship from flying apart? It's a 26-hour-a-day job, and I don't see anybody else stepping up to help. I have to take Stimugen just to keep up with repairs."

"Really?" Mintax asked. "What was that device you were working on before you destroyed it?"

Her eyes flared in anger. "That wouldn't have happened if Goober had just left me alone like I told him to."

"What was it?" Mintax asked again, remaining calm in the face of her ire.

"It was a servo control module I picked up from our last re-supply run. I was trying to get it operational so we can finally upgrade our thruster control system, but I guess that's impossible now. Isn't it?"

"Did we need it badly enough for you to risk your health to repair it?"

"I—that's not the point."

Mintax moved closer to her and placed a gentle hand on her shoulder. "I think it is," he whispered.

Hitch shrugged off the large hand and jabbed an index finger into his chest. "You don't know anything," she insisted. "I wouldn't need to worry about repairs and upgrades if you would just stop trying to squeeze every damn credit you can out of this ship without regard to your crew."

The comment stunned Mintax. He contained his instinct to return fire, choosing to remain calm by considering Hitch's altered state of mind. "That's not fair, and you know it."

"Of course it is. You care more about making money than your crew or this ship. More than you care about me." She lowered her head and pounded her fist on Mintax's muscular chest. "Why don't you care about me? You're always so cold." She looked up and stared into his eyes. "Am I as replaceable to you as that module?"

Mintax usually kept his distance from emotional issues, but this was one time his guard was no match against the pain he saw in the eyes of the woman standing before him. He placed both of his hands on her shoulders. "You know that's not true."

"How do I know? You never tell me how you feel. We never talk about us. Don't you like me?" She ran her hand down the length of the orange shirt stretched tightly against his chest.

Mintax knew her emotions were erratic and unpredictable while under the control of Stimugen. Her words and actions weren't her own, and he had no intention of allowing her to do something she might regret. He reached for her hand and pulled it away from his body, but continued to hold her fingers softly in his. "You're not in control of yourself right now. We can talk about this again when you've had a chance to get some sleep."

She yanked her hand out of his grasp. "It's always later and never now. Well, I'm tired of later." She pressed her body against his, wrapped her arms around him, and planted her lips firmly against his.

Mintax was taken aback by the unexpected action and didn't immediately respond. He quickly found himself enjoying the kiss, feeling himself pulled into her presence. After a few seconds, he remembered that her mind was still altered by the drug, and her actions weren't truly her own. He placed his hands gently against her shoulders and pushed her back, separating their bodies. Regret immediately flowed through his mind as his body continued to yearn for her touch, but he cared far too much about his friendship with her to take advantage of her weakened state. "We can't do this," he insisted, gently pushing her away. It was an attempt to persuade himself as much as it was to convince her.

Hitch lowered her arms, saddened at the rejection. She looked at the deck and nodded.

He placed his finger under her chin and gently lifted her head to gaze into her eyes. "We will talk about this when you're not influenced by Stimugen. I promise."

She smiled wanly. Her close connection with him negated at least a part of the ill effects of the injectable sleep drug. "I'll hold you to that."

He smiled back, although he remained uncomfortable at the thought of addressing the situation again. He hoped her memory of recent events while under the influence would fade after a long, deep sleep. "Let's get you to bed."

She raised her eyebrows in mock surprise. "Oh?"

He slowly shook his head. "You know what I mean."

Hitch sighed. "I'm afraid I do." She looked across the room at the exploded module. "I'll clean this up first."

She began to move past him when he lightly gripped her arm. "I'll take care of the module. You just worry about getting some sleep."

"You're not going to tuck me in?" She smiled playfully while gazing into his concerned eyes.

"I think you can manage that on your own."

"Maybe, but it's definitely not as much fun."

Mintax shook his head and pointed to the door. "Would you get out of here already?"

"Fine." Hitch sashayed over to the exit and paused. She turned back toward him and lowered the opening of her tan, long-sleeved top to the middle of her chest, revealing a modest amount of cleavage. "You know where I'll be if you change your mind."

After she had left the room, he stared at the closed door. He wasn't immune to her uncharacteristically provocative actions and had to shake his head to clear the thought before collecting the pieces of the broken module.

DISCOUNT DINNER

Steve, the Starcruiser Galaxy's weapons specialist, held a spoon full of green and purple mush a foot away from his face, peering at it skeptically. He rotated the visibly unsavory entrée, examining it from all sides in search of alien life signs. "So, you say you got this stuff at a discount, huh?"

Captain Mintax tore his gaze from his own plate of mush and narrowed his eyes at Steve. "Look, it's the best we could get on our budget. Of course, if *somebody* hadn't jettisoned our last cargo haul into space while we were still in warp to Hassa Station, we would've had a few extra credits to spend on something better."

Andre "Goober" Gu'ber, the ship's communications specialist, glanced around the polished, metal table at the disappointed expressions of his friends. "Well, you told me to have the cargo moved near the door so we could have it ready to go when we arrived at the station. All I did was set the payload beams to do the work before going to lunch. That's all. I swear." He held his right hand in the air as if to verify his honesty.

"I said *to* the door, not *out* the door." Mintax shook his head in annoyance.

Goober offered a weak smile. "I guess I should have examined the console instructions more carefully, huh?"

"Yeah, I guess you should have," the captain said.

Glenda "Hitch" Ritan, the ship's engineer, knew from experience Goober's mistake was simply that, and she quickly changed the subject to save him from further condemnation. "So, what exactly is this stuff anyway?" She raised her left eyebrow at the goo when it undulated almost imperceptibly on her plate.

"It's cheap," Mintax replied. "That's all I need to know."

Goober grabbed his plate and stood. "I'll have Jonn scan it to find out."

"Uh. No, thanks," Steve said. "I think the less we know about it, the better."

Goober shrugged. "Okay. Let me know if you change your mind." He sat back down and adjusted the position of his triangular-shaped plate on the table.

Hitch sighed. "If nobody else is brave enough to try it out, I guess I'll be the first."

"Good luck, babe," Steve said. "I think you're going to need it."

Hitch looked at Goober and smiled weakly. She inhaled deeply and forced her hand to plunge the goo into her mouth.

The rest of the Galaxy's crew waited breathlessly for Hitch's reaction as the goop sloshed around in her mouth. A tiny, hard bit slithered across her tongue, attempting to evade her throat. Hitch's tongue caught the object and moved it toward her teeth. It crunched audibly when she bit down on it.

"So, what do you think?" Goober asked, breaking the suspense-filled silence.

She paused for a moment, doing her best to control a powerful gagging reflex as the slimy substance slid down her throat. "Well, I've had worse."

"Really?" Steve asked in disbelief. "I find that hard to believe. Nothing I've ever come across looks even remotely as bad as this."

"What did it taste like?" Goober asked.

Hitch opened her mouth to reply, but thought better about responding directly. "Well, it's hard to describe. You'll just have to try it out for yourself."

Goober nodded. "Okay." Without another word, he shoved a heaping spoonful of the substance into his mouth. After struggling to swallow the goo, he smiled. "Mmm, not bad."

"Yeah, right," Steve said. "I don't buy that for a second."

"You're wrong," Mintax replied. "We did buy this, and it's all we're going to get until we get paid for our next job. I suggest you get used to it."

"Ha," Steve said. "That's easy for you to say. You haven't even tried it yet. Let's see what you think of it before you try to pass it off as an alternative to starvation."

The captain gritted his teeth, but didn't reply. Instead, he dipped his spoon into the goo and separated a large quantity of it from the rest of the swelling mass. With a cold, hard gaze burrowing directly into Steve's eyes, Mintax moved the spoon toward his own mouth. Before the captain could jam the utensil into his face, his wristcom chirped.

Without hesitation, Mintax dropped the spoon back onto his plate and activated his wristband.

"Captain, could you come to engineering for a minute?" Jonn asked. "I want to show you something."

Hitch stared uncomfortably at her plate of goo and quickly turned her attention to Jonn's holographic image above Mintax's wrist. "It sounds like I should go too." She removed a white napkin from the collar of her tank top and stood. "We'll be there in a minute."

"No, no, that's okay," Jonn said. "It's just something I want to share with the captain. Thanks for the offer though." He smiled nervously through the electronic connection.

Hitch twitched her nose and slowly sat down.

Steve smiled. "Nice try, babe. If I have to eat this stuff, so do you."

Hitch picked up her spoon and plunged it back into her food. "I thought he needed help. That's all." She did her best to contain a grimace when she lifted the utensil to her mouth.

"Right," Steve said.

Mintax casually glanced at his plate. "I'll be right there." He stood and moved swiftly toward the exit.

"I'll put your plate back in the refrigerator for when you get back," Goober said. "I wouldn't want your food to get warm."

"Thanks," Mintax said in a low voice before exiting the lounge.

Steve watched Goober stand and collect Mintax's plate. "You wanna take mine too? I'm a little full." He slid his plate across the table toward Goober.

"Full of it, maybe," Hitch said sternly. "What was it you said, 'if I have to eat this stuff, so do you?' That means you too." She pointed her loaded spoon at the weapons specialist.

Steve sighed. "Fine." He pulled his plate back in front of chest. "I didn't want the captain to eat alone when he got back, so I thought I'd save some for later. Honest." He winked at Hitch.

Hitch shook her head. "Uh, hu."

* * *

Jonn paced in short spans two feet away from a glowing cylindrical device connected directly to the Starcruiser Galaxy's Infinity reactor. He did everything he could to bypass a localized force field blocking access to the yellow and purple object, but was unsuccessful in his attempts.

Captain Mintax entered engineering and

approached Jonn. "What was so urgent I couldn't finish my lunch?"

Jonn stopped his pacing and inhaled deeply. He turned slowly to face Mintax. "This couldn't wait. I...accidentally activated it when I tried removing it." He spoke in measured words, doing his best to control the flow of information. "It just happened, captain. Honest. I had no idea what it was until it was too late."

Mintax frowned at Jonn. "What are you talking about?"

Jonn pointed to the glowing device. "It's a bomb designed to act as a self-destruct mechanism, captain. It activated when I touched it with my spanner. There was no way to know what it was."

"We don't have a self-destruct device aboard this ship. I checked before I bought it."

Jonn wrinkled his brow and stepped closer to Mintax. "That's what I thought too. At least that's what the schematics told us. But there it is." He pointed to a one-foot-wide, square opening in the reactor's housing.

Mintax stepped past Jonn and knelt in front of the reactor. He peered inside the opening and saw a yellow, fluctuating light sealing off access to the cylindrical object inside. "How did that thing get in there?"

Jonn shrugged. "I'm not sure. Before the force field activated, I managed to scan it. Captain, it's built entirely from materials foreign to the Galaxy's construction. Someone had to install it after the Galaxy left the shipyard."

"And you activated it?" Mintax said in a controlled tone.

"It wasn't my fault. I was checking backup systems, and I couldn't detect the reactor's tertiary power flow modulator. When I opened the panel to check it out, I found that." He stared forlornly through the force field.

"And then you activated it?"

Jonn shook his head vigorously. "No, that's just it. I scanned the device and then tried to open a small compartment on its side. That's when it emitted a loud, annoying sound and activated the force field. I barely pulled my hand out of the way in time before the field went up."

"How do you know it's a bomb?"

"My scans picked up a Vuratium core. I haven't seen the material used in any practical applications because of its volatility, but it was the main element of high-yield explosive devices used by the Blue Circle a few decades ago. You know, the anti-Tioran Federation group?"

"Yeah, I know who they are."

The device emitted a whirring noise and a faint purple light. The light pulsed slowly in regular intervals.

Jonn's eyes opened wide in shock. "Oh no. That's not good."

Mintax narrowed his gaze at the opening. "So how do we stop it?"

"I'm not sure. I've never encountered this design before. Hold on." Jonn activated his wristcom. "I'll check the network and see if I can find out anything more about it."

The purple light's flashing interval increased almost imperceptibly.

"That light just sped up," Mintax said. "How much time do we have?"

Jonn bit his lower lip. "I can't be exactly sure, but based on my analysis of its increasing power output, I'd say it'll reach critical mass in about 30 minutes, give or take."

"Figure out how to fix this and get it done," Mintax moved toward the exit. "I'll tell the rest of the crew and prepare for evacuation in case you fail."

* * *

Steve lifted a spoonful of goo to his mouth. "Well, here goes nothing." He gradually inserted the spoon into mouth. When he wrapped his lips around the utensil and extracted it from his mouth, he barely contained his body's urge to vomit.

"Ahh, this stuff is horrible," Steve spat. His tongue popped in and out of his mouth, attempting to wipe away the taste by scraping it against his teeth. "I've had gun cleaner better than this crap."

"It's better than nothing," Goober replied, looking on the bright side of a bad meal.

Steve dropped his spoon onto the plate of goo in front of him and sat back in his chair, moving as far away from the foul-tasting stuff as possible without leaving the table. "That's your opinion." He shivered at the sight of the offending food.

"My tongue feels furry," Goober said with minor difficulty. He readied his fifth spoonful of the substance and lifted it to his mouth when he paused and felt his lips with his free hand. His now purple lips ballooned to twice their normal size. "My mouth feels funny too."

Hitch cleared her throat. "Yeah, so does mine." She stuck out her tongue and looked down at her reflection in the polished surface of the table to examine it. Her lips were purple and twice their usual size. The normally pink tongue that protruded from her mouth had also become purple and sported a thin layer of fur amidst a bluish sheen of saliva.

Steve's jaw dropped in surprise. "Oh, that's just great. So we're going to look like that for the next week?"

"We'll manage," Mintax replied when he walked toward the table.

He stared in shock at Hitch's face for a second before continuing. "We have a bomb on board the ship, and unless Jonn can stop it, we need to be out of here in 28 minutes before it explodes. Steve, Goober, gather essentials and prepare to evacuate the ship in the shuttle. Hitch, head to engineering and give Jonn a hand. He's going to need all the help he can get."

"What!" Hitch said. She stood and stared at Mintax. "How did that happen?"

Mintax shook his head. "We don't know much about it, but it looks like someone planted it there not long after the Galaxy was constructed. Hurry, get down there and try to disarm it. We don't have much time."

Hitch nodded. "I'm on it." She dashed out

of the lounge.

"I'd better go too," Steve said. He stood and walked toward the exit. "Nobody knows more about bombs on board this ship than I do."

"Fine," Mintax said.

Goober stood and watched Steve leave the room. "Can I go too? I might be able to help."

"There isn't much either of us can do, Goober."

"Support is just as important as expertise, captain. We should be there for them in case, well, in case we don't get another chance." Goober looked forlornly at Mintax.

Mintax considered Goober's words. "You're right. Let's go."

Goober moved toward the exit, paused, and ran back to the table. He grabbed his plate of food and ran through the exit.

Mintax raised his eyebrows as the teen rushed past him.

"In case we don't make it, I'd hate to see this go to waste," Goober said.

Mintax shook his head and exited the lounge.

* * *

"No, that's not going to work," Hitch said.

Steve pulled a silver blaster from a holster strapped to his leg. "We'll see about that." He fired at the force field protecting the bomb, but the yellow energy shield absorbed the blast.

"See, I told you!" Hitch yelled in frustration. "Now put that thing away before you get us all killed."

"Damn thing!" Steve kicked the force field.

The combination of impacts caused the bomb's light to flash faster, emitting two pulses per second.

"You sped it up! Are you happy now?" Hitch asked.

Steve folded his arms. "Not really, no."

Mintax entered engineering with Goober in tow.

Jonn pointed to a 2x3-foot holographic display generated from his wristcom. "According to this information from an old database, the rate of the bomb's flash indicates we have about two minutes until detonation."

"That's it, everybody out," Mintax ordered. "We're evacuating the ship."

Hitch shook her head. "It's too late. There isn't enough time for the shuttle to escape the blast radius of the reactor." She moved closer to Mintax and looked up at his concerned face.

Mintax gazed into Hitch's brilliant, hazel eyes and slowly raised his meaty hands to grip her upper arms.

"It says here the Vuratium core draws its power from a separate source," Jonn said. "That's probably our reactor."

Mintax gently squeezed Hitch's arms before letting go. He moved next to Jonn and peered at the screen. "Will shutting down the reactor stop that thing?"

"No, Captain," Hitch said. "The device's failsafe would instantly detonate its core."

Steve looked at the hourglass-shaped reactor housing. "Can we cut into the metal around the opening and access it that way?"

"The force field extends completely around the device," Jonn replied. "That wouldn't work."

"Not completely around it," Goober said. He thrust his spoon into the plate of mush and pulled out a heaping mass.

Mintax turned to Goober and narrowed his eyes. "What do you mean?"

Goober jammed the spoon into his mouth, pulled out the empty utensil, and pointed it at the reactor. "If the bomb is getting power from the reactor, then it can't be sealed off completely, can it?" The mouthful of goo partially muffled his words.

"Jonn?" Mintax asked.

Jonn tapped on his control screen. "He's right. The device is connected to a power and coolant line, exactly like the power flow module it replaced. It not only gives the bomb all the power it needs, it also allows it mimic the functions of the module, masking its true nature from our sensors."

"How can we use that information to stop it?" Steve asked.

Jonn frowned. "I'm not sure."

"One minute until detonation," Hitch said. "There just isn't enough time to stop it."

Goober moved another spoonful of goo toward his mouth when he paused and looked at an access grate in the deck next to the reactor. He looked at his plate and then moved to the grate. Balancing the plate carefully in his left hand, he opened the grate with his right. The lid clanged to the deck, drawing the crew's attention.

"Goober, what are you doing?" Hitch asked.

Ignoring Hitch's question, Goober pulled a metal handle on top of a round cap. A hissing sound filled the room followed immediately by steam. He pulled the cap off a metal pipe and dropped it on the deck. Wasting no time, he positioned one of the three corners of his plate into the pipe's opening and watched as his food slipped inside.

"Are you insane?" Steve asked. "You can't put that crap in the ship. It'll gum up the works!"

Goober resealed the cap and stood. "Yep. Exactly."

Jonn tore his gaze away from Goober's experiment and watched his control screen. "Maybe it's not such a crazy idea after all. That coolant access pipe leads directly to the bomb."

"What will that do?" Mintax asked.

"We're about to find out," Jonn said.

The crew watched as a schematic of the pipe system on Jonn's screen showed Goober's mush entering the bomb. Sputtering and a loud grinding noise followed soon after that. Three seconds later, the bomb emitted a small pop and deactivated, taking the force field offline.

Goober clapped and cheered. "Woohoo! It worked!"

Steve looked dumbfounded at the opening in the reactor. "I don't get it. Nothing we did could stop the darn thing, and then Goober comes along, drops his lunch in it, and it quits. How does that work?"

"Apparently, the bomb's Vuratium core doesn't react well to whatever was in that food," Jonn said. 'Good job, Goober."

Goober beamed a smile at Jonn. "Thanks!"

"See, Goober's cargo accident wasn't so bad after all. It saved our lives," Hitch said.

"I guess," Mintax said. "Now will someone get that bomb out of there and off this ship?"

Jonn shut down his control screen and moved toward the reactor. "I'll take care of it. It's the least I can do for activating the device."

Hitch looked at Jonn's dejected expression and elbowed Mintax in his ribs. When the captain looked at Hitch, she motioned her head toward Jonn.

Mintax sighed. "It wasn't your fault, Jonn. Someone put that device on the ship long before either of us was born. We were bound to stumble across it sooner or later."

"It was put there a lot longer before he was born than you, Captain," Goober corrected. He smiled brightly at Mintax.

Mintax grumbled.

"We should probably go finish our lunch and get out of Jonn's way." Hitch grabbed Mintax's hand and pulled him toward the exit.

"Maybe afterward, we can see if the food

will grow hair on your head, Captain, just like it did on our tongues," Goober suggested. "It might turn your head purple, but at least you wouldn't be bald anymore."

Steve's eyes opened wide in disbelief. "Well, that's my cue to get out of here. Nice knowing you, kid." He dashed out of engineering.

A flash of anger sparked in the captain's eyes.

"Thanks, Goober," Hitch said. "Maybe you should stay here and help Jonn. He might need it."

Goober saluted to Hitch. "Okay. I will." He trotted back to the reactor and watched Jonn insert a spanner into the reactor's housing.

"Come on," Hitch said. "You can join me in the lounge. It's been a while since the two of us had the place to ourselves."

Mintax softened his gaze and nodded. "Yeah. I'd like that. The company, not the lunch."

Hitch smirked. "Who said anything about lunch?"

DISTANT DISCOVERY

"Sixty seconds until warp bubble collapse," Jonn announced. The Galaxy's programmer and backup navigator wasn't looking forward to this assignment. As far as he was concerned, the sooner they finished it, the better. He turned in his green chair at the navigation console and peered back at Captain Mintax. "There's still time to back out if you want to." He put on the most encouraging smile he could muster.

Mintax shook his head, refusing to back down. "This is the first paying job we've had in weeks. Unless you have another way to pay for food and spare parts around here, we're sticking to the mission."

"I still don't know why they picked us for it," Goober said. The Galaxy's science and communications expert swiveled in his chair at his console to face the captain. "Doesn't the Tioran government have their own ships they could send instead of paying us to do it?"

Steve grunted in amusement. "We're investigating the status of a scientific outpost near a black hole. Sending us in is a lot cheaper than risking the loss one of their own shiny ships." The Galaxy's weapons expert was particularly fond of missions involving gunplay. The promise of a payday, if there is one, was merely a bonus.

"I guess that makes sense," Goober said.

"Actually, it doesn't," Hitch corrected. The Galaxy's engineer knew that intentionally getting anywhere near a black hole was never a good thing. "I told you this was a bad idea from the beginning, and I still haven't changed my mind."

Steve smiled in reassurance at his crewmate. "Maybe you will after we get paid. Didn't you just say we needed a new power adapter for the environmental control system?"

"Yeah. So what?"

"Well, I'm not sure about you, but I'd like to keep breathing for a while longer. If this mission will help make that happen, I'm all for it."

"Don't you mean as long as you get a chance to test the new targeting system upgrade to blow something up?"

"A guy can dream. Can't he?"

"Dropping out of warp now," Jonn announced.

The Galaxy slipped out of warp and into normal space inside a solar system with a single planet orbiting a red dwarf star. A gray, elliptical observation station orbited the lonely barren world.

"Captain, I think I know why the station hasn't reported in recently. Look." Goober transferred a close-up visual of the station to the main viewscreen.

Deep, black scorch marks and a heavily pitted hull dominated the station's appearance. Small chunks of its enhanced armor shielding floated uselessly in space, leaving sections of the station exposed to the frozen vacuum if its surroundings.

"Shields!" Mintax yelled.

"Online, Captain," Steve said, salivating at the chance for battle. "Powering up weapons."

The Galaxy's heavy blasters extended from their mounting points. A green glow emanated from the barrels of the weapons, ready to engage any threat that dared to move within range of their brutal reach.

"Any other ships in the area?" Mintax queried.

"Not that I can tell, Captain," Goober responded, "but if there are any, interference from the black hole isn't going to make finding them any easier."

"Stay on it," Mintax ordered. "What's the status of the station?"

Goober checked a holographic display of the damaged lab. "Most of it still has power and life support, but I wouldn't want to get too close to the living quarters."

"Why not?" Hitch asked with concern.

"They're gone," Goober replied. "Whatever attacked the station took out the crew too."

"Maybe they used the escape pods to get out of there," Jonn postulated.

Goober nodded. "Maybe, except that the pods are still there, and…" His voice drifted off.

"Go on," Hitch encouraged.

"There are six bodies floating in the debris field around the station," he continued.

"How many people were on the station?" Mintax asked.

Goober checked the station information packet transmitted by the Tioran Federation. "Eight."

"It looks like we've got two missing scientists," Steve announced. "How much do you want to bet that whoever did this still has them?"

"I'm more concerned about why."

Hitch shot an incredulous glance at Mintax for his cold reaction.

He noticed her disapproval and sighed. "There's nothing we can do to help them unless we know where they are. The best way to find that information is to figure out what went on at that station."

Her rigid posture softened. "Then I guess we're going to the station."

He raised his palms toward her in a placating manner. "Hold on. I didn't say anything about you going over there. Goober and I can handle this. I'll need you and the rest of the crew to stay here, in case whoever attacked the station decides to return."

Hitch folded her arms indignantly. "Nobody knows more about coaxing information out of control systems than I do. I'm going, and that's final."

Mintax opened his mouth to protest, but realized that the conviction flaring in her eyes left little room for debate on the matter. "Fine, but if anything happens, I want you back on this ship immediately. Got it?"

"Sure, and I'll be right behind you when the time comes."

He growled softly. "Let's go. Steve, you have the bridge."

"Fine with me," Steve replied, hoping for combat action to test his superior skills. "I'll try to save a few pieces of the invaders for you as souvenirs, if they return."

"You mean after you rescue the scientists?" Hitch corrected.

"Sure," Steve smirked, showing little conviction in rescuing the captured personnel.

Hitch scowled as she entered the intra-ship transport chamber.

* * *

"What's that smell?" Goober asked. He sniffed the air that lurked in the station's control center. A light haze filled the room, masking some of the more devastating damage to its control systems.

"Fried circuitry," Hitch replied. "It looks like whoever attacked the station tried to destroy its internal systems to hide whatever they were looking for."

"Or make sure nobody else got their hands on it," Mintax added. "Does that mean we're wasting our time here?"

Hitch smiled casually at him. "There hasn't been a system invented yet that I can't repair or crack." She moved to one of the damaged consoles and began repairs.

"I guess that's a no," Mintax muttered. He turned and made his way to the exit. "Come on, Goober. Let's check out the rest of the station for any clues the attackers might have left behind."

Goober dropped a smashed yellow console fragment on the ground and stepped cautiously around the debris scattered on the deck to follow. "Coming."

* * *

Back on the bridge of the Galaxy, Jonn noticed a faint shimmer in the light of distant stars. He squinted at the main viewscreen to get a better look at the phenomenon, but the distortion disappeared as quickly as it appeared. "I don't like this. I think something's out there."

Steve poked through the display menu of Mintax's command chair controls, adjusting them slightly for greater weapon control accessibility. "You're just being paranoid. Whoever did this is long gone by now."

Jonn pinched his eyebrows together in contemplative concern. "Maybe. We should probably keep the shields up, just in case."

"Are you kidding me? There's a black hole out there. You just try and stop me from keeping them up and see what happens."

"No, thanks."

The shimmering effect appeared once again on screen.

"Did you see that?" Jonn asked.

Steve stiffened his relaxed posture in the command chair. "Yeah, I did. Tell the captain we might have company out there. He might have to cut his vacation a little shorter than he expected."

* * *

Mintax deactivated his communications link with Jonn after a briefing on the situation and opened a connection to Hitch. "It's time to pack up and get out of here. It looks like we might have company."

"Almost done," Hitch said, distracted. "Just about there…got it!" she cheered in triumph. "I'm bringing the computer core online now."

"Fine. We're on the way back to you.

There's nothing around here but useless, broken equipment."

Goober thrust his hands into his pocket and extracted a collection of small, multi-colored crystals. "I wouldn't say that, Captain. I found all of these great games and movies in the rec room. I figured the scientists didn't need them anymore since they were, you know...out there." He pointed to an adjacent window into space.

"Whatever," Mintax dismissed. "Hitch, download whatever you can from the core, and be ready to move out when we arrive."

"Got it." She deactivated her communication link and studied the station's holographic command interface. The large display streamed a massive quantity of scientific research related to the black hole as the core uploaded to the Galaxy's computer.

"The transmission is coming through perfectly," Jonn said across the station's now repaired communication system.

"Good. I'll keep an eye out on things from here," Hitch said. She studied the information flowing across the display, gleaning what she could from the complicated mess when she spotted a disturbing set of instructions. She opened up a second holographic window from the main screen and called up the information she had just seen. As she read the data, her eyes opened wide with concern.

When Mintax and Goober entered the control room, she jumped in her seat, startled out of her deep, trance-like concentration on the control screen.

Mintax narrowed his eyes at her. She usually didn't startle easily, and he immediately knew something was wrong. "All right. What is it?"

"Captain, we have to stop the download," she replied. "They were doing much more on this station than studying the black hole. They were developing technology to replicate its destructive power into a weapon. Nobody should have this type of power, Captain, not even the Tioran Federation."

"They're paying us a lot of money to retrieve this data, Hitch. I'm going to need a damn good reason not to collect it."

She stood and moved directly in front of him. "How about the lives of trillions of people, because that's exactly what's at stake if technology like this falls into the wrong hands, as it always does. We can't allow that to happen, Captain. The price is too high, no matter what they're paying us."

Mintax rubbed his chin as he mulled over the information.

"It's okay if we don't make any money, Captain," Goober added. "I can make do with the food stores we've got on the ship for a few more weeks. I can be pretty creative in the kitchen when I have to be." He flashed a smile at his captain.

Mintax cringed at the thought of some of Goober's previous creativity in the galley when he didn't have much to go on.

Hitch placed her right hand on Mintax's left forearm. "We'll be fine, Captain. We always find a way to make do."

"Well, you'd better make do with getting your butts over here," Steve announced over the station's communication system. "A gunship just decloaked near the station, and it's locking its weapons on you. Get out of there, now!" Steve roared.

"Stop the upload," Mintax ordered. "Set the station on auto-destruct, and do it on the move. We're getting out of here."

The station rocked from the force of heavy torpedoes slamming into the durable but not indestructible station armor. Lights and console illumination aboard the station flickered as the crew made their way to the small shuttle bay.

Jonn transferred the communication link to Goober's wristcom. "Hurry. The station's hull is crumbling. I'm not sure how much longer it's going to last."

"Won't they fire at the shuttle when we undock?" Goober asked. He panted slightly as he and the others ran down a narrow corridor toward the shuttle bay.

"Just worry about getting your butts back to the ship," Steve said confidently. "I'll keep those bastards busy while you return."

The station rapidly disintegrated under the punishing force of the powerful torpedoes, scattering debris in all directions. The crew scrambled aboard the shuttle and sealed the hatch just in time to watch a massive pile of rubble crush the corridor they had just passed through.

Mintax quickly powered up the tiny craft and forced a rapid ejection from the shuttle bay without the assistance of the station's auto-dock/undock tractor beams. When the shuttle escaped the dying confines of the station, the powerful enemy warship's large gun turrets attempted to track it, but had difficulty following its tiny prey. The shuttle bobbed and weaved its way back to the Galaxy, avoiding the hyper-accelerated chunks of anti-matter launched in futility toward it.

Steve maneuvered the Galaxy toward the shuttle, attempting to close the gap to the rest of the crew as quickly as possible. He tried his best to distract the warship's turrets by firing all of the Galaxy's weapons at the much larger vessel, but the warship remained undeterred in its persistent attack of the shuttle's occupants.

With his keen piloting skills, honed after years of battle experience, Mintax guided the shuttle into the hangar of the Galaxy. When the warship's prey vanished inside the belly of the green starcruiser, it refocused its massive weapons on the stalwart vessel protecting its previous target. While it may have had a difficult time tracking the shuttle, the warship's turrets proved more than capable of reaching out to punish the Galaxy.

"Shields at 65 percent, Captain," Jonn announced after Goober, Mintax, and Hitch entered to the bridge.

Steve returned to his weapons console and did his best to target any vulnerable critical systems he could find aboard the attacking warship. "I'm barely scratching their shields, Captain," he yelled in frustration, trying to be heard above the many explosions going on around them as torpedoes detonated against the Galaxy's shields. "We'd better get out of here while we still can."

Hitch shook her head. "No, we can't. If

that ship escapes with the black hole technology, the entire universe is at risk of destruction."

"I'm open to suggestions," Mintax said in a rush. "Any ideas?"

The crew remained silent as the warship, four times the size of the Galaxy, continued its onslaught.

"Shields at 40 percent," Goober announced after returning to his station.

"There's no choice, Hitch," Mintax said. "We've got to go. Jonn, engage the engines. Take us out of here."

"Wait," Hitch yelled. "I've got an idea."

"Jonn, hold," Mintax ordered. "What's your idea?"

Hitch redirected her gaze to Jonn. "Do you still have a link with the station?"

He checked his console. "Yes, for now. Why?"

"They managed to build a black hole generator prototype weapon a few weeks ago," she explained. "My guess is that's what attracted the attention of our friends out there. Anyway, I think I can access it remotely to destroy that ship."

"Are you kidding me?" Jonn asked in horror. "There's a chance using a weapon like that could destabilize the fabric of space in this system, not to mention gain the attention of that black hole out there. If that happens, we'll be sucked inside and torn apart when it reaches out for us. That's suicide."

"If that happens, we'll still have a chance to warp away while the gravitational pull of the black hole reaches out for us," Hitch corrected. "We'll be able to escape before it can trap us here."

"Even so, this system will still be destroyed forever," Jonn insisted. "There's no coming back from that."

"The planet's uninhabited," Steve said. "Besides, nobody comes out here anyway. That's why the station was built here in the first place, in case things went wrong, which they did."

"Shields collapsing," Goober announced.

"Do it," Mintax ordered. "Jonn, get us out of here the moment you see any change in readings from that black hole."

Jonn wasn't a fan of destroying an entire star system, but he realized the alternative could be far worse if they failed to act. He took a deep breath and blew it out. "All set here, Captain."

Hitch accessed the station control systems remotely and tapped into the prototype device.

The ship rocked from the explosion of a barrage of hybrid weapon and torpedo strikes slamming into the Galaxy's hull.

"Hull at 75 percent," Goober announced.

"The weapon is almost fully charged," Hitch yelled. "I'm targeting the warship, now."

"What about the missing scientists?" Goober asked. "Aren't we going to rescue them first?"

Mintax pursed his lips together resolutely. "I'm sorry, Goober, but we can't. We don't stand a chance against that ship, and we can't let it get away. This is our only chance to stop it."

"Besides," Steve added, "they're probably already dead anyway. There's no sense in having us join them."

Goober's shoulder's sagged in disappointed. "I understand."

When a green triangle flashed on Hitch's control screen indicating the black hole weapon was ready, she hesitated for a moment. She wasn't sure if Steve was right about the scientists, and she didn't want to be the cause of their deaths.

"Hull at 38 percent," Goober announced. "If we don't do something quick, I don't think we're going to have to worry about what's for dinner tonight."

With no other choice, Hitch pressed the activation button. "Firing now."

A massive, barely visible distortion wave projected from the station and enveloped the warship. Within seconds, the large vessel rapidly broke apart at the molecular level.

"I can barely see the beam," Steve commented.

"It's not in the visible spectrum of light," Jonn explained. "Since it's based on the dynamics of a black hole, that's one of its advantages. The target doesn't have a clue what's going on. By the time the enemy realizes there's a problem, it's too late."

Steve grunted his disapproval. He appreciated the satisfying explosion of an enemy ship, and wasn't exactly thrilled about having his prey fade quietly into oblivion. "How long is that supposed to take?" he asked.

"Less than a minute," Goober replied. "Look." He pointed at the viewscreen.

Only a cloud of dust particles remained of the large warship. The mist-like residue of the ship slowly faded away as it dispersed into the depths of space.

Steve sighed. "Well, that's disappointing. I was hoping for something a little more satisfying."

"Not getting our ship blown up is satisfying enough for me," Mintax insisted. "Is there any response from the black hole?"

Goober shook his head. "No reaction, Captain. I think we're okay."

"Not after the station self-destructs," Hitch amended. "We should probably go before that happens."

"How long until it self-destructs?" Mintax asked.

She checked her wristcom. "Another 22 minutes."

"Speed it up," he ordered. "I want to make sure it's gone before we leave."

She hesitated to follow the order. "Captain, now that the threat is gone, maybe we should try to adapt some of the non-lethal research on the station. Not everything they were developing involved weapons."

"You were right the first time when you said the research should be destroyed," Mintax replied. "I don't want anything from there falling into the wrong hands, and from my point of view, that means anyone."

After a few moments of contemplation, she finally agreed. "You're right. I just thought we might be able to make the work of those who died on the station count for something."

"We did," he insisted, "when we took out that ship. Those criminals will never be able to harm anyone again, and I doubt we could have done it without the efforts of those scientists."

She smiled. "That's a good sentiment, Captain. I think they'd appreciate it." She refocused her attention on her wristcom and tapped a sequence of commands on its holographic control screen. "Five seconds until detonation."

"Now, Jonn," Mintax ordered.

The Galaxy's stardrive engaged just as the station exploded. The blast lasted only a moment before the station caved in on itself, eventually taking the planet and the sun along with it.

"So, do you think the Tioran Federation will still pay us for the mission?" Goober asked.

Steve laughed in amusement. "Those cheap bastards? We'd be lucky if they don't charge us for the loss of their research."

Mintax shot an expectant look at Hitch. "Speaking of which…"

She nodded. "I almost forgot. I'll purge the data now." She tapped a command sequence into her wristcom and watched a progress indicator on its screen while the computer deleted the information from the Galaxy's core. When the computer finished deleting the data, a pop-up window appeared indicating that it moved a single file from the research collection to a subdirectory in Hitch's wristcom. She quietly deactivated the screen and smiled at the captain. "That's it. All research from the station is gone."

"Good," he replied. "Now we can focus on how we're going to pay for food and repairs."

"I've got an idea, Captain."

Steve turned in his seat to give Goober his full attention. "This, I've got to hear."

Goober frowned in admonition at Steve for a fraction of a second before smiling at Mintax. "Well, we still have the general information the Tioran Federation gave us about the station, so if we sold it back to them, we might get enough to pay for what we need."

"And why the heck would they do that?" Steve asked. "Out of the kindness of their cold hearts?"

Goober shook his head. "Nope. They'll probably want the existence of the station wiped from all records because of what they were researching, especially since it didn't work out so well. If we have information that proves the station existed in a system that just got swallowed by a black hole…"

"Then they might be willing to pay us to keep it quiet," Mintax finished. "Good idea."

Goober stuck his tongue out at Steve, who rolled his eyes in response.

"I'm going to get started on repairs," Hitch announced. She moved toward the intra-ship transport chamber. "Let me know when it's time for dinner."

"You've got it," Goober replied.

After Hitch had moved into the chamber, she couldn't help but feel a tingling sensation of anticipation as she thought of working on a key piece of technology downloaded from the station. The important discovery would provide the ultimate upgrade to the ship, and it was doubtful that she'd receive any measurable sleep until the project was complete.

DAMAGE CONTROL

"Well that was easy," Steve said with derision. "What else can it do, train people to kiss their rear ends goodbye if they ever get attacked by pirates?"

A wave of disappointment washed over Jonn at the ineffectiveness of his latest creation. The Galaxy's programmer designed a Damage Control Training program that simulates battle damage and repair aboard a starship. He intended to create, and sell, the program capable of providing a starship's crew with a real-time training tool that could help them work more efficiently in an actual battle situation. During its initial test, the program proved too simple a challenge for the Starcruiser Galaxy's battle-hardened crew, and wasn't marketable to a mass audience.

Jonn tapped furiously on an engineering console, doing his best to prove the value of his program to the ship's weapons specialist. "Hold on a second. I think I know what the problem is."

"I think it worked fine," Goober said in support of his friend. The Galaxy's quirky, but brilliant science and communications specialist thought the restroom malfunction simulation wasn't much of a challenge, but he didn't want to make his friend feel worse about the program than he already did. "Good job." He gave a 'thumbs up' to Jonn.

"Please," Steve scoffed. "I had a harder time getting to second base on a date last week, and believe me, that wasn't much of a challenge." He smiled smugly at his crewmates.

"Didn't you come back early that night because of an…equipment malfunction?" Goober asked with an innocent look on his face.

Jonn raised a questioning eyebrow.

Steve widened his eyes in surprise before he turned to Jonn. He noticed an amused smile on the programmer's face. "It's not what you're thinking," Steve quickly explained. "The captain needed me to get back to the ship to fix one of the weapon turrets. The damn thing wouldn't retract after a scheduled automatic diagnostic test, and he needed me to coax it back into place."

Jonn snickered. "We certainly wouldn't want to cruise around in space with your weapon hanging out. Would we?"

Goober giggled at the comment.

Steve wasn't amused. "Yeah, very funny. So how's that useless program of yours coming along? Is it going to simulate battle damage in the kitchen next? Maybe it'll choose to cause a malfunction in the waste reclamation system. We all know how crucial that is to repair during a battle."

The sharp comment instantly wiped away the amused look on Jonn's face. "You really want to know what it can do? Here, I'll show you." He tapped a short keystroke sequence on the control panel.

Deafening emergency alarms echoed throughout the spacious engineering room as the lights dimmed to 20 percent of capacity.

Jonn turned to Steve and folded his arms. "Let's see if you can figure this one out on your own."

Steve narrowed his eyes for a moment before he moved to an engineering console.

He studied the display and noticed a power disruption in the reactor. The supremely confident weapons specialist laughed. "Really? That's all you could think of?" He shook his head. "I'll have this fixed in ten seconds."

Jonn gestured to the console. "Go for it."

Goober watched as Steve attempted to reroute power distribution to auxiliary systems. A look of concern swept across the man's face when he noticed a significant falloff in output readings.

"You should probably regulate the power flow through the capacitor relay before you inject it into the distributor," Goober suggested.

"Thanks, but I think I know what I'm doing." Steve continued with his plan to restore power to the ship. "Besides, it'll take too long to send it through the relay. We need full power to keep the blasters running in battle, and every second counts."

"Okay. If you say so." A twang of pleasure resonated in Jonn's voice. He stepped back a few feet from the man and motioned for Goober to do the same.

A moment after Goober moved next to Jonn, several small arcs of energy shot out of the engineering console Steve worked on and discharged into his hands. Steve immediately jumped back from the console. "Gaa! What the heck was that?"

"It was only a mild shock," Jonn explained. "That's the Damage Control program's way of saying you made the wrong choice." He took great pleasure in watching his pompous friend make a bad decision, a small form of vengeance for mocking his program a few moments ago. "You should have listened to Goober. Now you fused the injectors. It'll take an hour to repair the problem before we can fully restore power."

Steve massaged his aching hands and narrowed his eyes at Jonn. "You think that's funny? Let's see how your program likes this." He pulled a silver pistol from his holster, thumbed a button on its grip to activate its power core, and fired at the console. The unit exploded in a colorful shower of debris and electrical energy discharges.

Jonn's jaw nearly dropped to the deck in shock. "What the heck did you do that for?"

Satisfied with the results of his vengeance, Steve deactivated his pistol and put it back into its holster. "It looks like you're going to have to come up with a new training program."

"The program is on the mainframe, not the console," Jonn said in exasperation.

Steve shrugged. "Whatever."

"I think Hitch is going to be pretty mad when she and the captain get back from their trip and see this," Goober said.

Hitch, the Galaxy's engineer, had departed aboard a shuttle the previous day with Captain Mintax to attend a lecture on experimental planetary gravitational propulsion. They were due back in less than two hours.

"I guess you'd better start fixing it then, huh?" Steve said. He tilted his head up slightly in a righteous pose and moved toward the exit.

"Wait a second. You're the one who blew the stupid thing up," Jonn protested. "I'm not going to clean up after you."

Steve paused mid-step and turned back to face him. "Unless you want Hitch to get mad at you for messing up the reactor, you will."

Jonn stood his ground. "Not after I tell her you blew up the console because you got mad at it."

"Um, guys," Goober interrupted.

"What?" Steve and Jonn said almost in unison.

"I think we've got company." Goober pointed to a holographic display above an undamaged console.

The ship's scanners, operating on simulated

emergency power, picked up three frigate-sized vessels bearing down on top of the Galaxy.

"Why didn't the long-range scanners pick them up before they got the drop on us?" Steve asked.

Jonn sighed. "They're down from simulated battle damage." He knew he'd have to correct the issue in the next upgrade to the program.

"Well that's just great," Steve said. He moved closer to the data console and squinted at the display, scrutinizing the configuration of the potentially hostile vessels. "Ah, crap. What the heck are tech salvagers doing out here? I thought this place was supposed to be off the usual space lanes?"

"It's a dead star system, so it should be," Jonn replied. "They probably use probes to track down stray ships, and today, they happened to find us."

Goober peered at the holo-display and noted an unusual energy beam emanating from one of the salvagers. The beam wrapped around the Galaxy, bathing it a soft, blue light. "They're disabling our star drive," Goober announced. "I don't think we're going anywhere with that inhibitor beam locking us down."

"No problem," Steve replied in a calm tone. He walked over to an engineering console and switched it to a tactical configuration. "I'll just blast them with a quick burst from our turrets. Easy." He tapped a series of commands into the console to lock weapons on the offending frigate. When the system failed to engage, he furrowed his brow and turned to Jonn. "Would you turn this stupid program of yours off already? I can't engage the weapon systems."

"Um," Jonn hesitated. "There's only one way to turn it off, and that's by solving the simulated problem."

"It's just a computer program," Steve insisted. "You mean to tell me there isn't an off button?"

"I'm still working on it for the next upgrade," Jonn explained. "It's still in the alpha test phase, and I haven't gotten around to adding all of the planned features yet."

"Not being able to shut it down is one hell of a problem to put off until later," Steve said. "You don't think that maybe you should have figured that out *before* you turned it on?"

Jonn shrugged. "How was I supposed to know we'd get attacked while it was on? Besides, you're the one who was so bent on getting it up and running as soon as possible so we could sell it for, how did you put it, 'a quasar-load of credits.'"

Steve balled up his fists in frustration. "This shouldn't be a problem at all. It's just a stupid simulation."

"Not from the computer's perspective," Jonn said. "The problem is very real to the ship, and unless we fix it, there's no way to get primary systems back online."

"Well then fix the stupid *simulated* problem!" Steve yelled.

"It's not that easy, at least not anymore. When you damaged the system, you made the problem worse. I wasn't kidding when I said it would take an hour to fix."

Goober studied the holo-display of the salvage ships while Steve and Jonn were arguing about the finer points of programming when he noticed a potential solution to their situation. "Guys, according to our scans, I don't think their engines are built for speed. If we can just get power back to ours, I think we can outrun them."

"We can't even get enough power back online to run maneuvering thrusters," Steve replied in disgust. "How do you suggest we get the power we need to outrun those bastards?"

Goober tilted his head in contemplation while studying information pouring across the display screen. "We can do it if we use your solution to route power to the engines."

Jonn's eyebrows pinched together in a concerned expression. "You can't be serious. The ship would explode halfway through the startup sequence."

"Well, maybe not *exactly* like Steve's solution," Goober continued. "We can do it the right way, through the capacitor regulators, and then directly into the engines, bypassing all other systems. If it works, it should give us enough of a power boost to overcome their engine inhibitors, and they'd have no way of catching up since we'd be much faster than they are."

Jonn nodded while his mind worked through the power distribution setup they'd need to make the plan work. "As long as the engines don't blow up in the process, he's right. It should work."

"Fine," Steve said. "It beats the heck out of sitting here waiting to get salvaged to death. Do it."

Goober rushed over to the auxiliary navigation terminal to lay in a course for Gustastamine. "As soon as power is restored to the engines, I'll take us to meet up with the captain and Hitch. I bet they'll be pretty surprised when they see us on the planet. I just hope they don't get too mad when they find out what happened."

"They won't ever find out," Steve said in a stern tone. "We should still have enough time to put the ship back together before the conference is over. I don't want the captain holding this fiasco over my head the next time he thinks about leaving me in charge."

"That's good," Goober agreed. "I don't think he'd ever leave us alone on the ship again if he found out."

A loud, high-pitched noise suddenly filled the room. The crew quickly covered their ears, but their efforts did little to dampen the brutal, penetrating sound.

"What the heck is that?" Steve shouted to be heard over the noise.

"Their salvager beams are trying to break up our hull," Jonn yelled. He moved quickly to an engineering console and began rerouting power to the engines. "If we don't get out of here in the next 30 seconds, the ship is going to break apart."

Goober cracked his knuckles and wiggled his fingers. "I'm all set here."

Droplets of sweat formed on Jonn's forehead as he concentrated on his work.

"Just a few more seconds. There. Go!"

Goober shook his head. "I can't. The drive is still spooling up."

A massive amount of small, particle-sized fragments of the Galaxy's hull began peeling away from the ship in a fog-like mist and toward a nozzle collector mounted underneath each of the frigates. After a few tense moments, a flashing, green triangle illuminated on Goober's console. He immediately pressed it, launching the Galaxy forward in a forced, emergency warp. The unexpected move by the Galaxy prevented the frigates from deactivating their salvagers before their target activated its star drive. The salvage beams automatically retargeted the only source of material they could find, sucking in the high-energy output of the Galaxy's warp emission. The dangerous energy feedback caused the salvage control systems to overload. One by one, the expensive reclamation equipment aboard each of the frigates exploded, disabling all three vessels.

"Whoo-hoo!" Goober cheered. "We made it."

"What's the damage to the hull?" Steve asked in concern. He feared it would be too extensive to repair before the captain returned to the ship.

Jonn studied a damage report scrolling across his screen. "Fortunately, not much. The salvage beams took off a thin layer of the hull, but the nanite system is already working to repair it. We also managed to avoid damaging the engines with the forced power transfer. I *think* we'll be okay."

Steve exhaled audibly. "That's a relief. How long until we reach the planet?"

Goober checked his console. "We should be there in a little under two hours."

"I'll have the Damage Control simulation fixed by then." Jonn gestured to the remains of the console destroyed by Steve. "Why don't you work on replacing the console? I think they'd notice if it still looks like *that* when they get back."

Steve grumbled. "Fine, but if you ever get me in a bind like this again, you're on your own cleaning it up."

"Me?" Jonn asked in irritation. "You're the one that said creating the training program for a quick profit was a good idea."

"What do I know about programming?" Steve was confident in his blameless role on the project. "You should have known better."

Goober shook his head as the other two continued their argument. "Oh well. At least we've still got a ship to complain about," he said to himself. "Until next time, anyway."

DISTANT DISCOVERY II

Captain Mintax slammed his fist on the armrest of his command chair. "Those bastards screwed us again."

Goober, the science and communications specialist aboard the Starcruiser Galaxy, blinked in dumbfounded response. "I don't understand. Don't they want the material back?"

"It looks like they created a cover story for the research station's destruction," Jonn informed. The Galaxy's programmer scrutinized a Universal News Network report on the holographic screen of his console. He cleared his throat, preparing to read the short statement.

"In a tragic development, a devastating accident left eight scientists dead in a distant solar system. They were engaged in a vital research project to cure a virulent plague that wiped out the zeta colony on Ramius II earlier this year when an experiment lost containment and disrupted the station's reactor. Though the deaths of the heroic team members are a tragic loss, the Tioran Federation will persevere in its pursuit of a cure for the deadly menace that causes the deaths of countless millions each year." Jonn looked over his shoulder at Mintax. "That's it."

"Short, sweet, and full of B.S.," Steve commented. The Galaxy's weapons specialist laughed derisively. "That's the Federation for you. If you can't hide it, spin it into something positive."

Mintax grunted. "And why pay us to keep information on a highly classified research station secret when it's now publicly available?"

"Diabolical, yet typical," Steve quipped.

"It was worth a try." Hitch, the Galaxy's engineer, knew the Federation was unlikely to pay for essentially useless information, but she supported Goober's idea in the off-chance government officials were in a generous mood.

"For the trouble we went through to protect that station from pirates, we should have received at least some kind of remuneration," Jonn said.

"Maybe we would have if we hadn't blown up the station." Steve shot an accusatory glance at the captain.

Mintax gritted his teeth. "You know damn well we didn't have a choice. That black hole technology they developed would have been devastating to the entire universe if it fell into the wrong hands, and I wasn't about to let that happen."

"Besides, they don't know *we* blew it up," Jonn added, supporting the captain's decision. "As far as they know, pirates did it."

"They had no intention of paying us one way or another," Hitch asserted. "We got screwed again by the Federation, so let's just move on."

Mintax growled at the reminder.

Hitch knew the captain was frustrated by the unfortunate turn of events and could use a rare piece of good news to help cheer him up. She had waited for the right moment to reveal the existence of a special project she started and continued developing since the encounter with the research station. There wasn't likely to be a better opportunity than now. "Captain, I've been working on something recently that I think will help make up for the lost income."

Mintax raised his left eyebrow in curiosity. "Oh? And what's that?"

She opened her mouth to reply, paused, and changed her response. "I think it's best if I show you." She extended her right hand to him. "Come on," she encouraged.

He hesitated for a moment but gave in. "I might as well. It's not like we have anything better to do until the next mission."

"Mind if I tag along?" Steve said smoothly. "I like a good surprise." He stood up from his chair.

"Not this time," Hitch said. She led Mintax into the intra-ship transport chamber and they transported away.

Steve narrowed his eyes at the closed door and sat down.

"What do you think it could be?" Goober asked.

Steve shrugged. "If it were anything useful, we would have heard about it before now." He wasn't pleased with Hitch's quick dismissal of his presence, and wasn't about to show any further sign of curiosity toward her surprise.

* * *

When they entered engineering, Hitch did her best to contain her excitement in anticipation of revealing the project to Mintax. The extra bounce in her step toward the Infinity reactor betrayed that intention. She gestured to the silvery, metallic hourglass-shaped housing of the reactor. "What do you think?"

He eyed the reactor for signs of alteration, but found none. He directed a skeptical gaze toward Hitch. "I don't see anything."

"Oh," she replied sheepishly. "Sorry. I'll bring it online." She activated her wristcom and tapped a few buttons on its holographic display. The alternating yellow and blue glow of the reactor immediately faded and the ship's systems switched to emergency power.

Mintax peered around engineering at the dull illumination of the crimson emergency lights and refocused his gaze on his engineer. "Hitch," he said in a cautiously drawn tone.

"Give it a moment."

After that moment, the reactor reinitialized, cycling through various shades of white before shifting to a color that could only be described as a dark, absence of white. Power to the ship's systems returned promptly afterward.

"What did you do to my reactor?" Mintax demanded in an accusatory tone.

"Something wonderful," she answered. "I've been working on a way to boost the output of the reactor, but I always came across the same issue—not enough reaction in the chamber. Every module enhancement I could piece together only produced marginal results until I found the secret sauce."

"Secret sauce," Mintax repeated dubiously.

"Yes." She hesitated. "You're probably not going to like this, but I kept the results from one of the experiments on the station."

He narrowed his eyes at her. "I told you to delete everything."

She held her hands in the air defensively. "I know, I know, but when I saw the results of the experiment, I realized it was the exact solution I've been looking for." She held her breath as she waited for his response.

He pursed his lips while mulling over her actions. Mintax gazed at the reactor, studying the unusual glow in the chamber. "How, exactly, did you *enhance* it?"

Hitch's expression brightened at his lack of accusation. "I wanted a source of power greater than what the Infinity technology provided. When I saw the alternative source in the station's database that didn't require significant alteration to our own reactor, I had to test it out, and it worked." She beamed a triumphant smile at Mintax.

He frowned. "Using any technology developed from the research of a black hole is dangerous, no matter how innocuous it might seem." He exhaled audibly, digesting the possibilities presented by the upgrade. "That being said, what kind of power boost are we looking at?"

A proud smile spread across her features. She accessed the control screen of her wristcom and studied a summary assessment of the ship's systems. "There's a 320 percent boost in power to the ship's general systems, a 450 percent boost in energy weapon power, a 655 percent increase in engine output, and an 810 percent boost in shield output. What do you think about deleting the technology now?"

Mintax's jaw involuntarily slackened at the astonishing news. "Hitch, the ship's systems can't take that much power. You'll blow us up the first time we try to use anything."

She shook her head. "I've already thought about that. I made adjustments to the flow regulators to make sure no system would receive more power than it could handle. The reactor is completely safe."

Jonn, Goober, and Steve burst into engineering and ran toward the two.

"Are you guys okay?" Jonn asked in concern. "There was a system-wide power disruption, and when we couldn't get the comms working, we thought there might be a problem."

"Everything's okay," Hitch insisted. "I was just showing the captain the new power upgrade I gave the reactor, and it's working perfectly."

"Why don't you warn us next time, babe?" Steve scolded. "How are we supposed to know what the heck is going on unless you tell us?"

Hitch conceded the oversight. "I'm sorry, guys. I just wanted Mintax to be the first to know about the upgrade. It won't happen again. I promise."

Steve folded his arms in indignation. "It better not."

"So, did it work?" Goober asked.

Hitch beamed at him. "Better than I could have imagined. Take a look at these readings." She placed the palm of her hand on the holographic image above her wristcom and pushed it off to the side. She placed her other palm on the image and separated her hands from one another, expanding the image. "If you'll notice the power boost to the weapons, Steve, I'm sure you'll appreciate the value of my work."

Steve's eyes opened wide with delightful anticipation, and he whistled a brief tune. "Holy crap. Would you look at that? We'll be able to take out a small moon with that much firepower."

Jonn wasn't as enthusiastic as Steve about the modified power output. "I don't get it. How could you have possibly boosted reactor output by so much?"

She shrugged. "I used a process developed by the scientists on the station. I know what you're going to say. I should have worked with you on the project, but it's something I've been interested in doing for a long time. That, and I enjoy working on projects by myself from time to time. I'm sure you understand."

"Actually, I don't." Jonn's face took on a grave look of concern. "This isn't good. Not at all." He accessed his wristcom and examined a reactor diagnostic screen.

Mintax furrowed his brow at him. His tentatively positive reaction to the upgrade immediately collapsed into trepidation.

"What's wrong now?"

Jonn closed his eyes and sighed. "Look at the power output on screen."

The crew turned to Hitch's display screen. Available power indicators slowly increased, reflecting a steady surge in reactor output.

"Isn't more power usually better?" Goober asked.

"Not when there's no way to stop it," Jonn answered.

"What exactly do you mean?" Mintax demanded.

Jonn pinched the bridge of his nose with his forefinger and thumb. "I mean if we don't find a way to shut down the reactor, it's not only going to destroy the ship, it's also going to rip apart this sector of space."

Mintax shot an accusatory glance at Hitch. "What is he talking about?"

A cold fear swept across Hitch's body. She manipulated the data displayed on her holographic screen and studied the energy reaction in the chamber. "This can't be right. They solved this problem."

"Apparently, they didn't," Steve said. "So, what's the problem again?"

Jonn frowned. "Captain, the reactor is using an artificial singularity to generate power, and it'll keep growing until it breaches containment," Jonn explained. "When that happens, anything in this region of space will be wiped out."

"Then shut it down, now," Mintax ordered.

Jonn's shoulders sagged. "I'm sorry, captain. I can't. There's no way to reverse a singularity once it forms."

Mintax turned to his engineer. "Was there any information in the research on how to reverse the process?"

"No," she said in a deflated tone. The magnitude of the situation numbed her mind.

"We could eject the reactor and get it off the ship," Goober suggested.

Jonn shook his head. "That won't stop the singularity. We have to find a way to force it to collapse in on itself, or at the very least, stop it from growing until we can figure out what to do with it."

Hitch snapped her head toward Jonn. "That's it." She looked at her control screen and began to tap furiously, entering a series of equations.

Jonn studied the data flowing across her screen. "Yeah. I guess that could work."

"What could work?" Mintax asked in irritation. He didn't enjoy being out of the loop on anything that had to do with the well-being of his ship.

When Hitch didn't reply, Jonn explained for her. "The engines can absorb and utilize most of the power from the reactor. If we crank up the output and tighten the shields to form a stabilizing skin around the ship's hull, I think we can drain enough of the reactor's power to buy us some time."

"How much time do we have if we don't?" Goober asked.

"About six minutes," Jonn replied.

"And if we do?" Steve wanted to know.

"More than six minutes," Jonn hedged.

Mintax grunted. "Great. I guess we have no choice then. Do it."

"There," Hitch said. "I've fortified the integrity of the engines to accept a higher velocity and modified the shields to protect the hull. We should probably get going."

"Where to?" Goober asked.

Mintax stared at Hitch's screen, studying the display. "As far away from civilization as possible. If we can't stop the reaction, we can at least try to contain the damage."

"You got it, Captain." Goober trotted out of engineering en route to the bridge.

Mintax directed his gaze at Steve. "You should probably go with him. I'll coordinate restoration efforts from here."

Steve nodded and looked at Hitch. If their

plan didn't work, this might be the last time he'll see his crewmates, particularly the lovely engineer. "You owe me dinner after this is over." He smirked.

Hitch smiled at his veiled confidence in her abilities. It was only a minor consolation after the colossal error in her decision to create the singularity. Her smile quickly faded as the severity of their predicament reclaimed her focus of attention.

"See you on the flip side," Steve said with optimism before leaving engineering.

When the engineering door closed behind Steve, Mintax returned his focus to Hitch and Jonn. "Do we have a chance at stopping this?"

Jonn shrugged helplessly. "I don't know, Captain. Scientists have studied singularities all their lives, and they're just now learning how to create one. There just isn't enough time to develop a way to reverse the effects."

Hitch's eyes opened wide with inspiration. "That could work." She tapped a series of queries on the control screen, accessing a mass of streaming data.

Mintax peered at Hitch's screen, but couldn't absorb the data flowing rapidly across it. "What is it?"

She didn't break her concentration from

the screen. "If we used the micro-QSR technology Jonn developed to wrap a time dilation bubble around the reactor chamber, I think we can reverse the time within it."

Mintax did his best to wrap his mind around the concept. "How exactly would using the Quantum Subspace Relocator help to eliminate the singularity?"

Jonn nodded rapidly in agreement with Hitch. "You're right. Captain, once a singularity forms, there is no known way to stop it, except for reversing time to prevent it from forming in the first place."

While Mintax was familiar with the concept, he was skeptical of the chance of success. "As far as I know, there hasn't been a successful reversion of a singularity before. Has that changed?"

"It will when we accomplish it," Hitch stated with confidence. "Jonn, grab the micro-QSR chip and install it in the reactor control module. I'll fortify the integrity of the chamber and set it for automatic shutdown when we've eliminated the singularity."

Jonn ran as fast as he could toward a hidden storage compartment across the room and retrieved the tiny chip. "Got it." He ran to the chamber and opened an access port. His eyes glanced up at a readout on the monitoring screen above the slot. "Oh crap. The integrity of the chamber is collapsing. It's only at 35 percent and falling rapidly."

"Just install the chip," Hitch said calmly.

Mintax glanced at Jonn and then at Hitch. "If we lose containment, will we still be able to shut it down?"

Hitch glanced at him before continuing her work.

"That's what I thought," Mintax muttered.

Jonn slipped the chip into an open slot in the reactor and backed away. The integrity readout decreased at a rate of 1 percent for every second that passed. "Hurry," he said. "Integrity at 20 percent."

Reactor chamber designers used lizanium, the same material as the Galaxy's hull, to create the housing more than 50 years ago. Though it's the strongest material known to modern science, it stood little chance at resisting the incredible pull of the singularity's growing gravitational force. A loud, painful groaning sound filled the air as concave indentations formed along the entire length of the chamber's housing.

"There. Activating QSR," Hitch announced.

The crew backed away from the chamber, preparing themselves for whatever happened next.

A white light formed around the reactor, swirling in a fluid pattern like clouds preparing for a heavy storm. Little could be seen of the reactor through the light as the intensity of its emission became blindingly impossible to witness. The crew shielded their eyes to block out the excruciatingly bright light. Within a few seconds, the ship shuddered and dropped out of warp.

The crew opened their eyes to the familiar dull glow of emergency lighting.

Mintax studied the disengaged reactor through the gloom and felt a wave of relief. "What's the status of the reactor?"

The pair examined the reactor readings on their respective wristcoms, followed quickly by a long sigh of relief by Jonn. "I think it worked."

Hitch nodded. "It did. The reactor is completely inert."

Budding concern quickly replaced the wave of relief that washed over Mintax. "Inert?"

"I'm afraid so," Hitch confirmed. "It'll take a few hours to restart normal reaction, but at least we're out of danger."

Mintax shook his head. "Not quite. Delete that singularity data, now." His stern voice left no room for questioning the conviction of his order.

"Yes, Captain." With a few buttons pressed on the control screen of her wristcom, she deleted the remaining data from the research station.

"Good," Mintax said. "Is there any damage to the ship?"

Hitch pulled up a visual display of the Galaxy on her holographic screen and shook her head. "No. All systems intact."

The captain rubbed his bald head and exhaled audibly. "Don't ever do something like that again without discussing it with the rest of us first. Understood?"

She lowered her head and nodded. "I'm sorry, Captain. I just wanted to enhance the ship's abilities and surprise you after the last mission went sour. It won't happen again."

Mintax noticed the pain of regret in her demeanor and knew her actions to improve the ship shouldn't be completely discouraged. He moved closer to her, placed a finger under her chin, and lifted it so her eyes would rise to meet his. "We're a team, Hitch. The next time you have an idea that could impact the rest of us, share it. We may not always agree to go forward with the idea, but it'll at least give us the chance to discuss it. All right?"

She wiped a tear from the corner of her

right eye. "I will. Thank you."

He smiled. "For now, I think you have a dinner date with Steve to get ready for. Don't you?"

Hitch sighed. "I think I owe everyone a dinner after today."

The captain nodded and turned toward the exit. "I'll collect another time."

"I'll hold you to it," Hitch insisted before Mintax left engineering.

"You don't owe me anything." Jonn inserted himself into her focus of attention. "I probably would have done the same thing if I had thought of it first."

"Thanks," she replied, "but I especially owe you. Without your help, we wouldn't be standing here right now." She moved toward Jonn and wrapped her arms around him in a tight hug. After a few seconds, she released him and kissed him gently on the cheek. "Thank you." She offered a warm smile before she moved toward the exit.

He blushed. "You're welcome," he called out as Hitch left the room. He enjoyed the sensation of her soft lips against his cheek, and wasn't averse to experiencing them again in the future.

DERELICT DISASTER

"Are you sure the ship is clear?" Captain Mintax asked. "I don't want any surprises if we go in there."

Goober, the Starcruiser Galaxy's science and communications specialist, studied sensor readings of the heavily damaged fighter carrier on his holographic display screen. "I don't see any energy readings coming from the ship, Captain. It looks dead."

"Looks can be deceiving," Mintax said.

Steve cracked his knuckles. "Then we'd better get in there and grab the loot while we still can. Their pirate buddies won't be too far behind."

"How long until they get here?" Hitch

asked.

"According to long-range scans, about 46 minutes," Goober answered.

Steve rubbed his hands in anticipation. "That's plenty of time." The Galaxy's weapons expert was always eager to get his hands on the latest in weapon technology. "Let's do it."

Hitch looked up from her engineering console and peered at him with a raised eyebrow. "Plenty of time?"

"Sure. We go in, grab the drone fighters, and get out before anyone spots us. Easy."

"When was the last time anything was easy?" Mintax asked.

Steve shrugged. "There's a first time for everything. Isn't there?"

"Yeah, like the first time our ship gets blown up while inside another ship," Hitch mocked.

"Come on," Steve said. "It'll take what, five minutes to get in there, fifteen to load up the drones, and another five to get out? We'll still have twenty minutes to spare before those pirates can even get close. That gives us a few extra minutes to thumb our noses at them before we warp away. No problem."

Jonn's quick, calculating mind, honed from years of programming experience, questioned

Steve's timetable. "I'm not exactly sure his math is accurate, but he's got a point. We can use the extra cash."

"I guess we could use the credits to replace the port shield emitter," Hitch agreed. "It's been acting up for a while, and bound to go out eventually."

Mintax exhaled in defeat. "Fine." He turned to Steve. "But if this goes wrong, I'm selling your gun collection to pay for a new emitter."

Steve threw his hands in the air. "Why me?"

"Because you're the one who suggested this. If anything happens, I'm blaming you."

Steve laughed. "Okay, and if we make it out alive, I think we should take some of the money from the score to buy that mine launcher I've been wanting."

Goober swallowed hard. "If?"

"Why a mine launcher?" Jonn asked curiously.

"I have a line on a sweet used launcher at a supply station close by. I've wanted one of those for a while, and this is the cheapest I've seen it. I had the vendor put it on hold while we finish the mission."

"And I'm sure he's a very reputable guy," Hitch added.

Steve shrugged. "As cheap as he's selling it, I didn't bother asking."

"Do you know how much mines cost these days?" Mintax asked. "How do you intend to pay for them?"

"That's not the point," Steve insisted. "We'll have a launcher in case we ever get our hands on some."

The captain rolled his eyes. "Great plan." He directed his attention to the Galaxy's programmer and acting navigator. "Jonn take us in."

The large hangar doors of the carrier offered more than ample space for the Galaxy's sleek, green hull to ease inside. Many of the fighter docking ports lining the inner perimeter of the hangar were smashed and scarred. Fragments of broken drone hulls, carrier structure fragments, and other debris floated haphazardly in the gravity-less interior of the carrier. The chaotic mess forced the Galaxy to move toward the end of the hanger on inertia and maneuvering thrusters only to avoid a crushing impact with the wreckage.

"There," Jonn said, pointing to the viewscreen. A mostly intact bank of drones rested comfortably in their docking slips at the end of a small, undamaged section of the hangar.

Mintax nodded. "Good. Tractor them in, nice and easy."

When the tractor system pulled the first drone away from its mooring, the drone's auto-nav system came online and requested targeting instructions from the carrier's combat interface and control system. When the CIC failed to respond, the drone sent telemetry data and a request for instructions to the carrier's internal defense system.

Though the powerful Slip-I reactor of the carrier was irreparably damaged, the IDS retained minimal emergency power in sleep mode. It activated on the drone's request, analyzed the data, and determined the Galaxy to be a threat. The IDS immediately restored partial power to the hangar by rerouting emergency reserves from backup life support. It sealed the outer doors of the hanger and ordered the drone to intercept and destroy the foreign vessel.

Jonn scrutinized the viewscreen and saw blue light from the drone's engines activate. The fighter writhed against the Galaxy's tractor beam, attempting to break free of the powerful hold. "Captain, I think the drone is attacking," Jonn said.

Mintax narrowed his eyes at the viewscreen. "I thought you said they were disabled?"

"I said the carrier's combat interface was destroyed," Jonn corrected. "I didn't say anything about the drone's weapon systems."

Mintax growled at the semantics. "Is that going to happen with all the drones when we pull them from their ports?"

"Unless we can take out whatever is still controlling them, probably," Jonn replied.

"The hangar doors just closed too," Goober added. "I think the ship knows we're here."

The single drone fired a furious blast of pulse beams at the Galaxy's tractor emitter. Without the starcruiser's shields, the fighter's weapons ripped through the unprotected emitter, releasing the small craft. The drone immediately flew in a tight orbit around the Galaxy, attempting to stay underneath the tracking ability of the starcruiser's turrets.

"Shields!" Mintax yelled.

"Done," Steve replied.

The drone pumped out as much damage as it could from its dual pulse cannons, but the Galaxy's shields proved far too powerful for its small weapons to penetrate.

"Is there a way to disable the drone without destroying it?" Hitch asked.

Jonn gave it some careful thought before

replying. "We could reduce the power output of our blasters to minimum levels so we don't instantly incinerate it. If we're lucky, we can target defensive and propulsion systems and take them out without destroying the drone."

"Are we going to have enough time to do that with all the drones before the pirate fleet gets here?" Hitch asked.

Jonn ran a quick calculation in his head. "We should have a few minutes to spare for a couple more, but it'll be close."

"What about the doors?" Goober asked. "Maybe it's just me, but it looks like they're going to be pretty tough to get through."

Mintax turned to his weapons specialist. "What do you think?"

Steve rubbed his chin, contemplating his options. "We don't want to use torpedoes, or we could cause a cascade explosion that destroys the rest of the carrier, along with us inside it. Our best bet is to ramp up power to the blasters and melt a path through the doors."

"So, we'll need even more time for Jonn to reconfigure the weapons to blast through the doors," Mintax concluded. "Now how much time are we looking at to recover the drones?"

"Not much," Jonn answered. "By the time we cut through the doors, we'll barely have enough time left to escape before the pirate fleet gets here."

"If we just take the one drone, that should be enough to pay for the new shield emitter. Won't it?" Goober asked.

"Barely," Hitch replied. "And that's if we go for an older model."

"Do it," the captain ordered.

Jonn nodded. "Taking weapons offline for reconfiguration."

"Steve, can you rig a torpedo to remote detonate?" Mintax asked.

"Hey, this is me you're talking to. Explosives are my specialty."

"What about the time you tried to blow open the lock on a sealed cargo container and blew up the container instead?" Hitch jabbed.

"Can I help it if I'm just too explosive for my own good? I could give you a personal demonstration later on, if you'd like." Steve winked at her.

Hitch rolled her eyes. "I'd rather take my chances with the explosives."

Mintax shook his head at the barbed banter. "I need that torpedo prepped and ready to drop on our way out *before* the pirate fleet gets here."

Steve stood and ambled toward the intra-ship transport chamber. "Yeah, yeah. I'm on it," he said before leaving the bridge.

"I've reduced power to the blasters by 90 percent, Captain," Jonn declared. "They're good to go."

"Finally. Hitch, take over the weapons station," Mintax ordered. "Target defensive systems and propulsion only. We need that drone intact."

"I'm on it." Hitch settled into Steve's chair.

The drone fighter valiantly threw as much firepower as it could against the Galaxy's shields when two bursts from the starcruiser's weapons quickly disabled it. Unable to defend itself, the drone sent a signal back to the carrier's IDS to report its status. Realizing the threat was greater than anticipated, the IDS sent an initialization signal to all remaining fighter drones.

"Uh-oh," Goober said.

Mintax didn't like Goober's 'Uh-ohs,' and this wasn't likely to be an exception. "What is it now?"

"I think the drone called his friends for help. The remaining drones are undocking. We should probably get out of here now."

"Fantastic," Mintax muttered. "Well, we might as well take out the damn things before we reset our weapons."

"Sorry, Captain," Jonn offered with

sincerity. "I took down the weapon system for reconfiguration again when Hitch disabled the drone."

Before Mintax could express his disapproval, Hitch spoke up. "The good news is the drone we disabled is safely in the shuttle bay. A small profit is better than none."

"We're not out of here yet," Mintax said. "How long until the pirate fleet gets here?"

"Just over ten minutes, Captain," Goober offered.

"Plenty of time, just like I told you," Steve assured as he reentered the bridge.

"Is the torpedo ready to go?" Mintax questioned.

"Of course. Now, if we had a mine launcher, we could have just hidden a few mines in the debris field and set them to detonate when the pirate ships arrived. But hey, that'd be too easy. Right?"

"Just drop the torpedo when we're ready to get out of here," Mintax ordered. "Jonn, where are my blasters?"

Jonn tapped a few buttons on his console. "They're online now, Captain."

"Good. Plot a reciprocal course out of here and get ready to pulse the engines when we've cut a path through the doors."

"I think that's my cue." Steve moved next

to Hitch. "You're welcome to stay in my chair if you're willing to sit on my lap."

Hitch quickly stood and clasped her hands together to prevent herself from strangling him. She forced a smile onto her face. "No, thanks." She strode back to her engineering console.

Steve shrugged. "Your loss." He sat in his chair and waited for the nose of the Galaxy to redirect itself toward the sealed hangar doors. "Here we go." He activated the Galaxy's forward cannons, concentrating their fire on a single point in the center of the doors.

A swarm of eleven drones established a tight orbit around the Galaxy, firing a barrage of micro-pulse lasers at the much larger craft. When the Galaxy unleashed its super-charged beams at the hangar doors, the IDS elevated its response to the threat.

Goober stared curiously at his control screen as the fighter drones actively scanned the Galaxy's shields. "Captain, the drones have stopped firing."

"It about time those things realized our shields are more than a match for their pathetic weapons," Steve said with smug satisfaction.

"I don't know," Goober hesitated. "They seem to be concentrating their scans on the port shield."

Mintax's eyes opened wide in concern. He knew the port shield emitter was only operating at minimal capacity. If it failed, the combined firepower of the drones might just have enough juice to damage the interstellar drive, stranding the Galaxy. He wasn't about to allow his ship to become easy prey for the approaching pirate force. "Steve, release the torpedo. It should make a nice surprise for our pirate friends."

"You've got it."

"Jonn, take the engines to five percent thrust," Mintax ordered. "I want to get as close to the hangar doors as possible when we've punched through them."

Jonn was about to protest the speed with a sizeable debris field blocking their path when the drones began firing at the port shield. Without at least some movement by the Galaxy, the drones would be able to apply maximum damage to the shield with zero mitigation. Jonn quickly activated the ship's engines.

The movement of the Galaxy caused the drones to recalculate their attack for optimum damage with only a ten percent loss in weapon efficiency.

"They're still on top of us, Captain,"

Goober announced.

"What's the status of the hangar doors?" Mintax asked.

Steve examined his weapons console. "We're 60 percent of the way through. Another minute should do it."

Without warning, a small explosion rocked the Galaxy.

"The port shield emitter just exploded, Captain," Goober informed. "They're targeting the engines now."

"Options?" Mintax asked.

"I say we use the ship as a battering ram and smash those drones one by one," Steve suggested.

"Any other options?" Mintax was hoping for something—anything—better.

Goober placed a contemplative finger against his lips. "What if we roll the ship on our way out? That could make it harder for the drones to target a specific point of attack."

"Make it happen, Jonn," Mintax ordered.

Hitch tapped on her engineering console and analyzed the mass and hull composition of the drones. "Maybe Steve has the right idea."

Steve raised his eyebrows in surprise. She rarely agrees with his ideas, and her support was highly unusual. "Seriously?"

"Not with our ship, but with theirs. I think I can use the aft tractor emitter as a type of remote control. It's crude, but I should be able to alter the trajectory of a single drone and use it to take out another."

"Do it," Mintax ordered. "That could take some of the pressure off our hull."

A drone circled around the Galaxy for another pass at the exposed drive system when the Galaxy's only remaining tractor beam snared the small craft. The drone's nimble thrusters tried their best to escape the hold, but all efforts proved futile as the tractor manipulated the direction of the fighter with ease. Against its will, the helpless drone careened toward two others in the swarm, disintegrating all three.

"Yes!" Jonn cheered.

"Nice job, Hitch," Steve concurred. "I'm impressed."

"Thanks," she preened with a smile. "How are those doors coming?"

Steve studied his combat control screen. "Just another second. There."

The intensely powerful beams of the Galaxy's weapon system deactivated when they finished burrowing through the hangar doors.

"Get us out of here," the captain

commanded.

The Galaxy's engines cranked up to 100 percent thrust. The hull of the starcruiser smashed through the drone debris field, taking moderate damage from bulky and jagged components. Just as the armor plating that protected the interstellar drive began to buckle from the drone attack, the Galaxy plowed through the hole in the hangar doors like a torpedo from a launcher. All drones still in pursuit desperately tried to fit within the tight space between the Galaxy and the doors while maintaining fire on their target. Without the logistics support of the carrier's CIC, none succeeded.

"Whoo-hoo!" Goober cheered. "We made it."

Mintax contained his cautious optimism at their escape. He continued his assessment of their situation. "What's the status of the drones?"

"All destroyed, Captain," Goober cheerfully replied.

Steve sighed. "Well, that's a shame. I was really looking forward to that launcher."

"That'll be the least of your concerns if we don't get out of here. Look." Hitch pointed to the main viewscreen.

In the blink of an eye, 16 ships dropped

out of warp almost directly on top of the Galaxy. Half of the fleet instantly targeted the resilient starcruiser while they simultaneously charged their weapons. The remaining forces moved toward the opening in the carrier created by the Galaxy.

"Warp us out of here, now," Mintax barked.

"I never did like getting attacked with my pants down," Steve remarked, referring to the destruction of the port shield emitter. He instantly knew the repercussion of his words and turned to Hitch for her pointed response.

She opened her mouth to reply, paused, and then shook her head. "That's just too easy."

Relieved at her restraint, Steve turned to the main viewscreen in time to watch the Galaxy warp away from the carrier just as a barrage of projectiles neared their former location.

"That was a close one," Jonn said in relief.

"Just the way I like it, especially when I can pull the trigger from a distance." Steve turned to Mintax. "Shall I?"

Mintax nodded.

Steve pressed a flashing red button on his console. "There. I feel better now. The torpedo might not destroy their ships, but it'll sure give them a headache for a while."

Goober looked around the room for a reaction. When nobody spoke up, he did. "So, how do we know if the torpedo worked?"

"I'm sure we'll be getting plenty of hate messages and death threats from them soon," Steve replied with confidence. "That'll be proof enough."

"I guess that good," Goober said with considerably less confidence than his crewmate.

Mintax pushed himself out of his command chair and moved toward the intra-ship transport chamber. "Tell me when we arrive at the station for repairs. I'm going for a workout."

"I think I'll go with you," Hitch said. She joined him in the transport chamber. "I can use a little stress relief right now." She looked at Steve, expecting a slimy comment.

Steve used every ounce of restraint he could muster to keep himself from asking her back to his quarters. "Have a good time." He aimed a brilliant smile at his attractive crewmate.

Hitch smiled at his obvious discomfort. "I will. Thanks."

"I'll watch the bridge if you guys want to take off," Jonn said to Goober and Steve. "I have to reconfigure the weapon system anyway, so there's no sense in keeping you here if you want to take a break."

"That's okay. I'll stay here and keep you company," Goober said.

"Not me. I'm out." Steve sprinted to the transport chamber and hopped inside. "I suddenly got the urge to go for a workout."

Jonn smirked. "It doesn't have anything to do with Hitch exercising in a tight outfit. Does it?"

With a sinister smile, Steve allowed the chamber door to close.

DECEPTIVE CARGO

The crew of the Starcruiser Galaxy stood in front of a large, five-foot tall gray cube in the center of the cargo hold. Red, glowing strips of light lined the edges of the container, highlighting the smooth, almost reflective surface of the cube. The Galaxy's crew recovered the curious oddity floating in a small asteroid belt just off a main space lane. Unable to resist the possibility of a profitable find, the crew hauled the cube aboard the ship for closer examination.

Jonn approached the cargo container with eager anticipation. He reached for a small control panel to activate its unpacking sequence when Captain Mintax grabbed his wrist.

"Wait," Mintax said. "I don't like this. Nothing is free in this universe, and I have a hard time believing someone *accidentally* left an expensive level V security container in the middle of a bunch of rocks." He turned to his weapons specialist. "Steve, scan it for hidden traps."

Steve nodded and stepped toward the container. "Let's find out what secrets this beauty holds." He activated the holographic control screen of his black wristcom band and typed in a sequence of commands. A glowing representation of the box appeared above his wrist with a horizontal scanning progress bar just below it. When the bar made its way to the right side of the display, the cube flashed green.

"Our luck was bound to change for the better, eventually," Steve said. "It looks clean."

Hitch crossed her arms and raised an eyebrow. The Galaxy's engineer knew better than to believe in pure luck, given their track record, and was hesitant to believe it now. "I still don't think this is a good idea, Captain. I told you we should leave this thing where it was, and I haven't changed my mind."

"You worry too much," Steve said.

"Sometimes you just have to go for it. After all, there could be a pile of credits in there just waiting for us to spend them."

Jonn studied the container, envisioning the possible contents that could be hiding inside. "I'm not sure about a pile of credits, but I'm willing to bet it has some interesting hardware in there." The Galaxy's programmer was always interested in new components for his special projects.

"I'll bet it's filled with StimCap," Goober surmised.

"StimCap." Steve parroted. "Why do you think that?"

The science and communications specialist studied the box. "The red lights along its side are the same color as my favorite drink. Maybe it got lost when the company was delivering a shipment to Delta IV."

Steve raised his left eyebrow at Goober. "Really? Is that all you have to go on?"

Goober shrugged. "It has just as much of a chance at being filled with StimCap as a pile of credits. Doesn't it?"

Hitch laughed. "He's got a point."

"I'll take my point over his, any day," Steve replied. "Mine makes me rich."

"Not if we just sit here staring at the damn thing," Mintax interjected. "Let's find out what's really inside." He nodded at his programmer.

Jonn approached the container and studied the control panel. Only three small, red and black buttons were visible from the outside of the container. "Without knowing the specific key sequence and length of the access code, it won't be easy to open this. The only alternative is to transmit a specific encrypted code across a high-frequency band to trigger the unlock sequence. Fortunately, I have a special hacking algorithm designed for just such an occasion."

The crew moved in close to watch Jonn's wristcom screen with eager anticipation. A vast array of multi-colored codes flashed across the display, deciphering the specific number, letter, and color combination of the key sequence. Within 30 excruciatingly long seconds, the program locked onto the correct sequence, flashing the key triumphantly on the holographic screen.

"Got it," Jonn announced. "Transmitting, now."

The red lights lining the container flashed slowly, picking up speed as the security locks retracted with a metallic scrape. After a few moments, the mesmerizing lights blinked out and the box began to unfold outward, exposing its contents for all to see.

Nobody moved for several seconds while the crew studied the unveiled object. A tan box with a multitude of black, angular grooves rested on the unfolded remains of its transportation container. The item, barely smaller than the cargo container itself, gleamed under the bright lights of the Galaxy's cargo hold.

"I don't get it." Goober's voice broke the thick silence hanging in the air. "What is it?"

Jonn let out the breath he didn't realize he was holding. He scanned the object with his wristcom, attempting to determine the answer to Goober's question. It was rare that he came across a piece of technology that he couldn't identify, and his curiosity became just as razor sharp as his focus on the unidentifiable item. "It has a power source, but," he paused. "This is strange."

Mintax's internal alert system flared with concern. "Explain."

Jonn studied the readings of the object on his wristcom. "It's made of kelitronium. My scans can't penetrate it, but I'm definitely picking up energy emissions. I'm going to try and trace it back to its control system to see if I can access it from the inside."

Hitch's eyes opened wide with concern at

the description of the object. "Captain, the only time I've heard about kelitronium being used anywhere was at Buzzart Industries. They tried designing a mining droid that could survive the atmosphere of a gas giant, but they never got a chance to test it."

"So, it's a droid then?" Steve asked, fantasizing about the opportunity to command it in battle.

"It is consistent with its configuration," Jonn agreed.

"I've never heard of Buzzart before," Goober said. "What happened to them?"

Hitch shrugged. "Nobody knows for sure. The research station exploded suddenly a little more than two years ago, and there were no survivors. The authorities determined the cause to be a meltdown in the station's reactor, but the people on the station should have had enough time to escape *if* that was the real cause."

"What about the project?" Mintax asked. "Did someone else take over?"

She shook her head. "There wasn't enough of the kelitronium material left to restart the project. Creditors eventually took what was left of Buzzart's assets to pay off the company's debts."

Goober glanced at the tan box and then

back at Hitch. "Do you think the container could have made it here on its own after the station exploded?"

"I doubt it," she said. "The station orbited a gas giant 55 light years from here. Unless the container has a hidden micro star drive system, someone had to intentionally drop it here."

Her explanation of the object was all the confirmation Mintax needed to hear. "Jonn, stop what you're doing. We're getting rid of this thing. Now."

Jonn tore his gaze away from the data on his screen and looked at him. "But Captain, I just got access to its control system, and it's more advanced than I thought. I should be able to use its own sensors to figure out how it got here."

Mintax was about to protest when a beam of light projected outward from the center of the tan unit to a point between the Galaxy's crew and the box. The light quickly formed into a life-sized holographic image of the notorious pirate Daro.

"Greetings, Captain," Daro announced with a gleaming smile. "I knew your crew would be smart enough to figure out how to open this box."

Mintax narrowed his eyes at the man who

tried to kill his crew on more than one occasion. "What do you want?"

Daro focused a sinister smirk at Hitch. "Well, I wouldn't mind having dinner with that lovely engineer of yours."

Steve moved a step closer to the hologram. "Just try it and see what happens."

Daro looked at Mintax. "Touchy, isn't he?"

Mintax folded his arms and glared.

Daro's smile faded. "You never were much fun. Fine. Let's get down to business. I have a special project I'm working on that will tip the balance of power within this sector of space in my favor, and I have no intention of letting you and your crew disrupt those plans, as you have in the past. I've decided to take the preemptive precaution of putting an end to your interference before it can happen."

"But how can we stop your plans if we don't know what they are?" Goober asked.

"That's not important," Daro snapped. "What is important is that I'll finally be rid of you and that ship of yours, once and for all."

Jonn surreptitiously continued his work on hacking the control interface of the droid on his wristcom.

Mintax beamed a penetrating stare into the man's cold, black eyes. "How did you know we'd pick up the container way out here?"

"How did I know you were going to go after free loot?" Daro inquired rhetorically. "Please." He waved his left hand dismissively. "All I had to do was bribe a few freighter captains and bartenders to track where you were headed. I simply planted the container where I knew you'd be, and sure enough, you took the bait. Your predictability really is your undoing." He redirected his attention to his right for a moment before returning his gaze back to Mintax. "Now, if you'll excuse me, I have other matters to attend to. I can't say I've enjoyed this last chat with you, Captain, but its finality pleases me to no end. Enjoy this parting gift with my compliments."

With a wink, his image disappeared. The droid immediately came to life at the end of the transmission, unfolding itself from its packaged configuration.

"Run!" Mintax roared.

The crew bolted out through the cargo bay exit and sealed the door behind them. Mintax activated the cargo bay control on the wall and watched with dread as the droid rose to its full height of three meters.

Shaped like a hulking humanoid, the droid raised its massive hands toward the cargo door. Its single, wide-angle golden eye glowed intensely while its hands retracted into its bulky forearms. When two wide-mouthed barrels replaced its hands at the ends of its forearms, diagonal lines along their shafts began to emit an eerie, red glow.

"Move," Mintax ordered, shoving his crew down the corridor.

A fraction of a second later, the cargo bay door exploded behind them. The force of the blast knocked them to the ground, briefly stunning them.

Mintax fought against a pain in his side and shook off the ringing in his ears to help his crew to their feet. When they made it to the end of the short corridor, he turned back just in time to see the droid step onto the remnants of the smashed cargo door in the hall. The hulking beast lumbered after them, scraping the walls of the corridor as it maneuvered its bulk through the restricted space.

"Captain, I've got an idea," Jonn said while he and the rest of the crew sprinted down the passageway. "If I can finish hacking the controls of the droid, I can stop it, just not for long."

"How long?" Mintax demanded.

The crew turned left at a T-junction, but not before the droid turned the corner at the other end of the corridor just in time to see which direction they went.

"We might have a dozen seconds or so," Jonn huffed, "while it reconfigures its defenses to block my connection." He took a breath. "After that, I can't stop it."

"What's that gonna do?" Steve panted dubiously.

"If we get it to the Stargazers Lounge," Jonn said between gasps for breath, "I think I can order it to take itself out."

"Why the lounge?" Goober asked when they rounded another turn.

"It's a large enough space," Jonn gasped, "and it's got an easy exit."

Steve huffed with skepticism. "I don't like the sound of that. Even if it works, it won't just hop in the transport chamber," he panted, "and follow us up five levels. How do we get it there?"

"I think it will work that out itself," Jonn said.

The ominous scraping echoed behind them as they continued to run. A green door with silver edges slid open when the crew approached the intra-ship transport chamber at the end of the corridor.

Mintax stared inside the chamber while contemplating Jonn's solution. He didn't like it, but he knew it was the best chance they'd have to stop the droid. "Get in."

The crew stuffed themselves inside the chamber just in time to see the droid lumber around that last turn. The immense Buzzart creation gouged massive grooves into the corridor walls as it moved with surprising speed. Without hesitation, the metal beast fired two red plasma rounds at its prey.

Jonn immediately tapped a sequence in the chamber control pad to enter their destination. The door closed and the crew transported away just before the droid's plasma fire ripped through the door and obliterated the chamber.

Using its advanced sensor system, the droid tracked the crew's location to a position several levels above. It analyzed the structural materials of the Galaxy, reconfigured its weapon system to an alternative setting, and fired dual tunneling beams at the ceiling. When the beams reached the same level as the crew, the droid deactivated its weapons and engaged a set of thrusters that extended from each leg. With slow, deliberate speed, the droid eventually made its way to the lounge level. When it landed on the deck, it deactivated and retracted its powerful micro-thrusters and began scanning the area. In less than two seconds, it detected the crew on the other side of the lounge door.

Programmed to eliminate the Galaxy's crew at all costs, the droid reconfigured its weapons once more and made its way to the lounge. Without hesitation, the mining marvel blasted through the lounge door and moved inside. Upon setting foot inside the room, Jonn immediately activated his control program.

The droid jittered momentarily as the program worked its magic, and within a matter of seconds, Jonn had full control of the beast.

"Let's go," Jonn yelled.

The crew dashed out of the lounge and ran toward a nearby crawlspace access hatch in the corridor. Mintax yanked the door open and ushered his crew inside. Once they were uncomfortably packed inside the tiny space, Mintax sealed the door behind him. "Now."

Jonn immediately pressed a pre-programmed command button on his wristcom display. Following its new set of instructions, the droid elevated its plasma cannons and fired at the ceiling's transparent armor.

The Highpoint Advanced Designs Corporation created the revolutionary armor in the lounge's ceiling as the perfect union between safety and ambiance in the former dignitary transport. It performed as well as the ship's lizanium hull, capable of withstanding substantial attack from external sources. The hull's strength from within the ship, however, was somewhat more limited. Highpoint later corrected the flaw in its future designs.

The atmosphere in the lounge and the exposed deck immediately rushed out through the newly created, gaping hole in the ceiling. The pressure equalization process jettisoned anything that wasn't bolted down to the deck, including the droid.

Jonn monitored the action from his control interface. "And…it's gone."

"Yes!" Goober cheered.

"Good," Mintax calmly replied. "Now, warp the ship out of here before that thing tries to get back in."

Jonn accessed the Galaxy's navigation system from his wristcom and ordered the ship to warp away.

The droid managed to regain control of itself just in time to watch the Galaxy enter light speed. Unable to deviate from its programming, the droid activated its thrusters and began a painfully slow pursuit of its prey, despite the improbability of its success.

* * *

Goober sulked in his chair on the bridge, saddened by the loss of his cooking gear in the lounge. "I just bought the last pan I needed for the full set of Jinvaro Tusani cookware, and now it's all gone." He sighed. "Do you think we can go back and get them later when it's safe?"

"No," Mintax replied in a stern tone.

Hitch tried to soften the impact of that response. "Don't worry, Goober. We'll help you replace them when we get the chance. Right, Captain?"

Mintax mumbled something unintelligible.

"Well, that bastard sure screwed us again. Didn't he?" Steve threw his hands upward.

Mintax clenched his fists and growled in response.

"What do you think Daro's plan is?" Hitch questioned the group.

"I'm sure we'll find out sooner or later, especially when he finds out that his pathetic attempt to kill us failed. Until then, we have a ship to repair." Mintax stood and turned to leave the bridge, pausing before he entered the transport chamber. "He was right about one thing."

"What's that?" Hitch asked.

"When we do find out what his plan is,

we're going to do whatever it takes to stop it."

Hitch smiled. "I was hoping you'd say that."

The End

EXCERPT FROM
THE VAMPIRE CLONES OF CLEGZ
CHAPTER ONE

Xeno swore under his breath. The culmination of his meticulous planning and carefully constructed extortions was blowing up in his face. Now, here he was, crouched behind a cargo container, hiding from the abominations that he and his partner Ju-Ka constructed in greed, and their chances for survival were dwindling by the second.

Xeno inhaled deeply and committed himself to the battle ahead, emboldening his resolve to take on his own malevolent constructs. He lifted his pulse rifle over the top of a large, orange cargo container and fired several wild shots toward a mass of dark figures at the other end of the poorly illuminated warehouse. The notorious thief checked the power level of his weapon and noted the encouraging amber "85 percent" glowing on its display. When he looked back at the approaching mass, two of the figures he thought he had already hit limped slightly, but continued their advance. He glanced down next to him. His partner of several years crouched next to him behind the safety of the crate.

"Any luck getting through?" Xeno asked.

Ju-Ka shook his head while staring at the "No Connection" message on the holographic display above his wristcom communicator. "Nope. I guess they're not at home."

Xeno frowned and continued firing at the approaching horde. "It's the atmosphere. There's too much interference to get a clear signal."

His peripheral vision spotted movement to his left. He swung his rifle around in time to see a pale, naked figure running toward him. The creature bared its razor sharp, gleaming white teeth as its red, glowing eyes locked on to a burst of green light pouring out of Xeno's gun. Its ghastly face laced with black veins disintegrated when a salvo of energy pulse blasts ripped into its ghostly white flesh. What was left of the body fell with a sickening thud to the metal floor in front of the two marginally successful entrepreneurs.

"Set the comm on auto-repeat, then help me take these things out. Hopefully, we'll catch a break and the interference will clear up long enough to transmit the signal."

"Okay." Ju-Ka set the auto-distress signal and pulled a black pistol from his waistband. He switched on its power core and peeked over the top of the orange crate. His silver eyes opened wide with surprise when he saw several dozen shadowy figures worm their way around various objects in the building, carefully avoiding Xeno's pulse fire.

"Can they do that?" Ju-Ka asked. "I thought they weren't supposed to have brains?"

Xeno emitted a disapproving growl and continued firing at the elusive figures. "I set the cloning process to remove all traces of intellect, but apparently the programming didn't take hold, at least not entirely. I guess the DNA from that vampire bastard was more resilient than I thought it would be."

One of the creatures moved too slowly to take cover behind a large, burned out and charred starship engine housing. Xeno seized the opportunity and fired at the abomination.

The energy blast severed the creature's left leg, forcing it to wobble on its remaining foot. It recovered quickly and leaped behind the protection of the metal object.

"You mean Clegz?" Ju-Ka asked. "Can't we just ask him nicely to have his clones let us go?" He fired a few shots from his pistol, uselessly striking the naked, severed leg lying on the ground.

Xeno directed a frustrated glance at Ju-Ka. "Can you at least shoot at the ones that are still moving?"

"Well, I didn't want it to get up and kick us."

Xeno shook his head, causing his black and purple mane to fall across his golden eyes. "Mission accomplished," he said, repositioning his hair behind his ear. "Now, keep firing." Xeno mowed down three vampire clones when they emerged from a stack of crates ten meters in front of their position. He squinted at what few figures he could see in the dim light. "Now that you mention it, I don't see the real Clegz anywhere. Where did he—?" His eyes opened wide with realization when he guessed the answer to his own question. "Did you lock the ship when you brought supplies back from Darnussian Station?"

Ju-Ka shrugged. "Maybe. I guess it sort of depends."

"On what?"

"Whether or not you're going to hit me if I say no."

Xeno grunted in frustration. "Dammit. Haven't I always told you to lock the ship whenever you park it?"

"Yeah, but there's nobody else on this moon. Who's going to steal it?"

The walls of the warehouse vibrated as the sound of an engine's thrust passed by overhead.

Xeno shot a menacing gaze at Ju-Ka.

"Oops. Sorry," Ju-Ka said with regret. He beamed a sheepish grin at Xeno. "I'll be sure to lock the door next time."

Xeno grumbled and checked the power gauge of his rifle. "You might not get that chance. I've only got 22 percent power left. What do you have?"

"Um," Ju-Ka muttered when he checked the power level of his pistol. Before he could reply, he spotted a one-legged creature hopping toward them from five meters away. He fired his pistol at the creature, striking it in the middle of its forehead. After it crumpled to the ground, Ju-Ka turned to Xeno. "That should just about do it."

Xeno stared incredulously at his partner. "What do you mean? You've barely even fired your gun. When was the last time you charged it?"

Ju-Ka rubbed the back of his neck while he struggled to remember. "Oh, maybe a few weeks ago, but I could be wrong."

Xeno lowered his head and pinched the bridge of his nose. "That's just great." He looked up and peered across the massive room at the approaching throng of vampire clones. "I guess we always knew this ride wouldn't last forever. Let's at least try to take out as many of these blood suckers as we can before we finish our run."

He pressed a sequence of buttons on the top of his weapon, switching it to full auto-mode, and opened fire at a medium-sized, wooden crate. The box exploded in a shower of splinters, revealing four creatures hiding behind it. Without hesitation, he fired another long burst of green energy blasts, reducing the hidden creatures to a pool of fleshy mess.

Ju-Ka eyed the large, sturdy crate that he and Xeno hid behind and rubbed his chin. "Maybe there's another way out."

To read more of this exciting adventure, go to http://www.starcruisergalaxy.com.

ABOUT THE AUTHOR

Rod has a passion for testing the limits of the improbable. His desire to explore the unknown is born from a love of science fiction that began when he was but a mere seedling on another plane of existence. Whether that consists of transcendence or daydreaming behind a desk is still a matter of heated debate.

Beyond a strong appetite for writing fiction, Rod also manages the fraud defense website ownyourdefense.net, blogs for several websites, and enjoys testing the tensile strength of gym equipment. When the construction of fantastic universes with his mechanical keyboard won't satiate his burning desire to create, a heavy set of dumbbells or learning a new fraud prevention technique will do.

To learn more about Rod's other cosmic journeys, be sure to check out www.starcruisergalaxy.com. While visiting the website, you'll find more information about the crew, puzzles, summaries of the Adventures of the Starcruiser Galaxy novels, as well as audio and video logs. You'll also find links to other exciting adventures with the Starcruiser Galaxy and its crew including the novellas *A Very Goober Christmas, The Wereghost Menace, The Vampire Clones of Clegz, and Brakka's Zombie Armada,* a collection of 12 short stories in *Galaxy Diaries,* as well as the novel *Who Blew Up My Ship.*

Dream big, and the universe will be your playground.

CONNECT WITH ROD:

Twitter: http://twitter.com/RodSpurgeon
Pinterest: http://pinterest.com/rodspurgeon
Facebook: http://facebook.com/Rod.Spurgeon
Website: http://www.starcruisergalaxy.com

GALAXY CHRONICLES
WORD SEARCH

M	P	A	O	I	X	A	X	P	V	R	G	C	S	I
V	Y	N	H	S	I	R	U	O	N	U	E	S	N	J
S	A	A	H	E	E	F	C	B	S	D	A	T	Y	D
N	E	M	U	I	N	O	R	T	I	L	E	K	E	K
S	Q	L	R	P	N	P	A	G	G	R	W	A	G	C
R	A	E	C	U	E	S	U	R	N	U	T	I	G	A
S	C	P	Z	A	T	E	U	A	E	H	N	I	J	L
K	C	S	I	A	T	O	L	L	F	M	E	L	W	B
M	W	A	M	E	H	N	P	S	J	O	M	I	T	P
I	I	I	R	J	N	R	E	S	S	H	P	Z	R	Y
A	N	N	B	A	U	C	S	T	M	H	I	A	A	G
E	B	A	E	P	B	Z	E	T	A	A	U	N	Z	A
D	E	R	E	L	I	C	T	J	O	S	Q	I	Z	B
J	C	H	H	C	E	R	T	O	S	S	E	U	U	L
S	H	O	V	R	E	S	H	Z	B	A	P	M	B	H

Black
Buzzart
Certos
Death
Derelict
Egg
Equipment
Gustastamine
Hassa
Hourglass
Internal
Kelitronium
Lizanium

Mine
Nano
Nourish
Purple
Rec
Sapience
Scarab
Servo
Sleep
Tentacles
Zeta

Scan this QR code for a helpful hint in solving the word search.

www.ingramcontent.com/pod-product-compliance
Lightning Source LLC
Chambersburg PA
CBHW021038130626
46552CB00005B/1907